Herbert Jackson Hapgood, Craven Laycock

Echoes from Dartmouth

A Collection of Poems, Stories, and Historical Sketches by graduate and...

Herbert Jackson Hapgood, Craven Laycock

Echoes from Dartmouth
A Collection of Poems, Stories, and Historical Sketches by graduate and...

ISBN/EAN: 9783744766050

Printed in Europe, USA, Canada, Australia, Japan

Cover: Foto ©Andreas Hilbeck / pixelio.de

More available books at **www.hansebooks.com**

ECHOES FROM DARTMOUTH:

A Collection of Poems, Stories, and Historical Sketches by the Graduate and Under-graduate Writers of

Dartmouth College

" For aught I know, he was of Dartmouthe."

EDITED BY

H. J. HAPGOOD, '96

AND

CRAVEN LAYCOCK, '96

HANOVER, N. H.

MDCCCXCV.

CONTENTS.

CONTENTS

ILLUSTRATIONS.

PORTRAITS.

INTRODUCTION.

COLLEGE life is full of sentiment. If a man is not aware of this fact while in college, he finds himself awakening more and more to the meaning of it as the years go by. The constant return of a graduate, in person or in heart, to his college, shows the force of the spell which is upon him. Alumni gatherings, which are becoming so large a part of academic life, are simply the tribute to college sentiment. These gatherings offer the occasion for the discussion of educational, and even public, questions, but they are the spontaneous outgrowth of a fellowship, which has but one origin, and which can have no equivalent. I doubt if all other agencies and influences combined are contributing as much to produce that fine sentiment, the tone and color so conspicuously lacking in American society, as our colleges and universities.

College sentiment has its literature. Apart from the well-worn reminiscence, or the familiar song, it finds constant expression in story and verse. College literature is not a matter of subject, but of atmosphere. Love, duty, adventure, the humor of life and its pathos, are the common property of the imagination, but every truest thing which is told or sung, is apt to betray its locality. That is one mark of its genuineness. This volume of "Echoes From Dartmouth," which takes its place beside others of like nature which have gone out from the College, will prove, I trust, no exception to the literary canon which has been recalled. I have seen little of its contents, for the volume is in press as I write this brief word of introduction, but the list of writers and of subjects, which is before me, insures a natural and pleasing variety. "Men of Dartmouth," by Richard Hovey, breathes in every line the spirit of the old College. It is a tribute and a challenge to the men who "keep the still North in their hearts." "Dartmouth in England," by Charles T. Gallagher, reproduces the delightful impression which the sketch made, as given by the author in the Old Chapel on the "Dartmouth Evening," September 17, 1895. "The Buildings of Dartmouth, by Robert Fletcher, brings to light, through careful research, a great deal of information which was in danger of passing out of reach, which had, in fact, passed out of the knowledge of many of those most familiar with the material history of the College. For the general selections made, and the arrangement of the volume, much can be assumed from the industry and taste of the Editors, Herbert J. Hapgood and Craven Laycock, of the present Senior Class —the Class of '96.

WILLIAM J. TUCKER.

DARTMOUTH COLLEGE, *November 11, 1895.*

DARTMOUTH CASTLE AND HARBOR.   See page 28.

Echoes · from · Dartmouth.

MEN OF DARTMOUTH.

MEN of Dartmouth, give a rouse
　For the college on the hill!
' For the Lone Pine above her
　And the loyal men that love her, —
　　Give a rouse, give a rouse, with a will!
　　　For the sons of old Dartmouth,
　　　The sturdy sons of Dartmouth —
　Though 'round the girdled earth they roam,
　　Her spell on them remains;
　They have the still North in their hearts,
　　The hill-winds in their veins,
　And the granite of New Hampshire
　　In their muscles and their brains.

They were mighty men of old
  That she nurtured side by side;
Till like Vikings they went forth
From the lone and silent North, —
And they strove, and they wrought, and they died;
  But — the sons of old Dartmouth,
  The laurelled sons of Dartmouth —
The Mother keeps them in her heart,
  And guards their altar-flame;
The still North remembers them,
  The hill-winds know their name,
And the granite of New Hampshire
  Keeps the record of their fame.

Men of Dartmouth, set a watch
  Lest the old traditions fail!
Stand as brother stands by brother!
Dare a deed for the old Mother!
  Greet the world, from the hills, with a hail!
    For the sons of old Dartmouth,
    The loyal sons of Dartmouth —
Around the world they keep for her
  Their old chivalric faith;
They have the still North in their soul,
  The hill-winds in their breath;
And the granite of New Hampshire
  Is made part of them till death.

                    R. Hovey, '85.

THE DARTMOUTH BUILDINGS IN 1803.

THE DARTMOUTH BUILDINGS IN 1803.

IT would be difficult for any of **the later** alumni **or** students of Dartmouth to realize how much change **a** century of existence has brought the college. A view **of** the three or four earliest buildings, **on** the south-east corner **of** the **common**, if such **a one** existed, would be **to** all entirely unrecognizable, and nearly so is the accompanying sketch of the second group. This is copied from a water-color belonging to the college, executed in 1803 **by George** Ticknor, afterward the famous Harvard professor, then eleven years of age. Evidently the details are inaccurate, but the general impression correct.

Then, as now, the most **important** figure **on** the knoll **was** Dartmouth Hall. **The vicissitudes of the esteem in which** this structure **has been** held are interesting **to consider.** Regarded at first with intense pride, **later eliciting** only a contempt which scornfully likened **it to** Noah's ark, it is now, **in its** battered age, once more **an object of** admiration, not only for the artistic beauty **of its** proportions, but **also for its historic** associations. **The** difficulties met **in its erection speak** plainly of the **early poverty of** the **college.** Planned in 1773, it could **not be begun for eleven** years, or finished for seven more, **although wood was** substituted for the brick of the **original design.** The £4,500 which **it cost, were raised** with extreme difficulty during a long period, in every possible way—by grants from the Provincial Assembly, private subscription, public lotteries, and the contraction of a debt which "rested many years, a hopeless drag on the prosperity of the College." Its early interior plan was very unlike that of the present time. On the ground floor a third transverse passageway ran through the centre, where is now the "Old Chapel," and a door at each end of the building admitted to a longitudinal corridor. In the second and third stories, respectively, the halls corresponding to this latter were bisected by a library-room and museum. This arrangement was very distasteful to the students, some of whom, in 1811, testified as much by blowing down the walls of the museum with a cannon, thereby nearly wrecking the whole building. A rather interesting scene occurred during the consequent disciplining. As President John Wheelock, according to custom, was announcing in chapel the expulsion of the principal offender and ordering him to leave the village within a specified time, that individual arose. "I shall go," he said, in effect, "when I judge proper." "Take care of that man," cried the President. "I am abundantly able to take care of myself," he replied. "Before I leave I shall tweak the nose of ——" (the person who had betrayed him). Thereupon he coolly turned and fulfilled his threat, then beat a triumphant retreat.

The building to the north of Dartmouth was erected by a Colonel Kinsman, and used by him while he was steward, and later by the College, until the system was abandoned in 1815, for a students' commons hall. The small house to **the east is the** original homestead of Eleazar Wheelock, the younger, which remained a private residence until it was torn down, sometime in the vicinity of the '30s. Its only connection with the College was from 1805–1807, when Ebenezer Woodward, its owner, attempting the stewardship, apparently kept **the** commons there. It **was** afterwards known as "the Acropolis," because it stood on the crest of the hill.

To the south-west of Dartmouth stands the chapel, measuring fifty feet by thirty-six feet, built in 1790, after the students had **torn** down the old "College Hall," in which the first place of worship was located. Half of the £300 which it cost was contributed by the townspeople, **who met** there with the students for devotional exercises **until their interest** was purchased by the College. **It was at first** open to the students for their entertainments, **but** later reserved exclusively for certain exercises **under** the supervision of College officers, which **included** even recitations **of the** senior class. It had **no chimney or** stove, and "here, **before** breakfast **on** the cold **winter** mornings and in **the dim twilight of the evenings,** muffled in their cloaks, officers and students gathered for prayers." It was removed **in** 1828 **to the present site** of the house formerly occupied by Professor Quimby **on** Main street, and was **used** by the townspeople **for prayer** meetings **until** the erection of **the present vestry, about** 1840, **when** it was transferred to **the lot on the north corner of** Main and Elm streets, **now the** property **of Mr. E. D.** Carpenter, and there **made** into a barn, in which condition it existed for many years.

The gambrel-roofed house at the extreme south of the picture is the final residence of the first president, the home, also, of Presidents John Wheelock, Allen (of the "University"), and Tyler, and,—for a year or **two**,— of President Lord. To make room for Reed Hall it was removed in 1838 to West Wheelock street, where it is now, in a considerably altered condition, the residence of Mrs. D. B. **Howe.** There is a tradition that its ell formed the **nucleus of the** present residence of Professor Richardson.

The condition **of the College at this** time was **precarious.** **The number of students, indeed,** was **about one hundred and twenty**-five, **including the** medicals, **but there were only four** professors, with **one** tutor, and the **total estimated income,** of which a **large** part **could not be collected, was $4,500.**

R. H. FLETCHER, '96.

MY CHOICE.

SHOULD some ethereal goddess come to me
  And offer whatsoever she could give;
Should heavenly voices whisper in my ear:
  "Take anything on earth you wish and live";
Should choice be given 'twixt honor, wealth, and thee,
  Which thinkest thou that I should likely choose?
    Would it not be thee?

H. S. BAKETEL, D. M. C.

RICHARD HOVEY, '85.

A CHAMPIONSHIP SONG.

RALLY, fellows, for a cheer! Victory's here!
　Bunch up, fellows, for a shout! Yell it out!
Join the wah-hoo-wah in chorus,
For the pennant floating o'er us.
Live the green and white forever;
Fade their ancient glory never.
Bunch up, fellows! Yell with me
For Dartmouth: One, two, three!
　　Wah-hoo-wah! Wah-hoo-wah!
　　Da-Da-Dartmouth! wah-hoo-wah!
　　　　T—i—g—e—r!

Louder, fellows, with your cheer! Do you hear?
Wake the noble Earl once more with your roar.
The laurel crown is ours again,
And shall be so while men are men.
The granite hills are at our back,
The wind's path our running track.
Bunch up, fellows, more and more!
For Dartmouth now a deafening roar!
　　Wah-hoo-wah! Wah-hoo-wah!
　　Da-Da-Dartmouth! wah-hoo-wah!
　　　　T—i—g—e—r!

2

Loud again the victory tell! One more yell!
Every Dartmouth man shall hear, far and near!
  While a heart with valor thrills
  We'll glory in the granite hills,
  And oft again, in victory's light,
  Shall float on high the green and white.
  Bunch up, fellows! One more yell!
  The green and white! Well—well—well!
    Wah-hoo-wah! Wah-hoo-wah!
    Da-Da-Dartmouth! wah-hoo-wah!
        T—i—g—e—r!

E. O. Grover, '94.

FRESHMAN: HOMESICK.

HE wonders what they're doing home tonight,
  And tries to plug beneath the smoky light.
Alas! How far his thoughts from vexing books!
How sad his air, how woe-begone his looks!
No carpets, chairs; all dull and bare and cold.
Is life worth living, after all? Tight roll'd
In quilts, he dreams—of going home some day.
Ah! homesick Freshman, your's the toilsome way.

G. A. Green, '98.

CLARKSON, RIGHT GUARD.

CLARKSON laid his curly brown head upon the Horace that was open on the table before him, and between the stubby fingers that covered his eyes a few drops of suspicious moisture trickled out. His parents and his classmates would have alike refused to believe it possible, but the fact was, Sam Clarkson was crying and feeling a good deal better for it, too.

Clarkson was the oldest son of a New Hampshire farmer. The swarm of little ones that came after him, needed for their food and raiment all that the rocky hillsides could possibly produce. So when Sam, infected with ambition by a winter's schoolmaster, announced his intention of going to college, his father gave him his blessing and plainly told him that was all the help he could expect.

With the pluck and perseverance of three Yankee generations in his blood, that did not daunt Sam in the least. He paid for his furnished room in a professor's house by taking care of the professor's horse and little garden; he waited on table at a dining-club for his board; secured a scholarship for his tuition; and was always on the look-out for small jobs, sawing wood, for example, to pay his few remaining necessary expenses.

All this had no effect upon his relations with his class-

mates. Thank Heaven, there was never a bit **of snobbery at** Dartmouth. When he made some brilliant "rushes" **in the first** recitations of the term, **the** men in his division **regarded him with mild** interest; but when, in the cane rush, he put the sophomores' best man squarely on his back and kept him **there,** then his **popularity** took **a** sudden and tremendous jump.

He was "old Clarkson" then to all the Freshman class, and nothing would do but he must play on their foot-ball eleven. Being a big fellow and a natural athlete, with muscles of steel, a clear eye and a well-controlled temper, Sam liked the game, and played **it in** a style calculated to bring terror to the hearts of his opponents. **It was** largely owing to his personal prowess **and inspiring** presence **that** the Freshmen kept the **Sophomores from scoring** in the **great** game of the **year, and the score stood** 0—0, while the whole college on the lines howled like mad.

When the alert captain **of the 'Varsity, seeing in Clark-** son **a** present excellent substitute, and a **prospective cen-** ter rush, or guard, asked **him to** come out **regularly with** the second eleven, he **was considerably surprised to be** met with a quiet but distinct **refusal.** "**I'm working my way** through," said Sam, "**and I** haven't time for **that** and my studies and foot-ball, too." Whereat the cap- tain grieved and **swore; but the coach, who** had **cap- tained the** first eleven **the College ever had, and** thought he knew Dartmouth men as well as he did Dartmouth foot-ball, **said:** "**Let him** alone. He'll get all the **plug- ging he wants in a year, and then he'll take to** foot-ball **like a duck to water. You** don't **need him** this fall, anyway."

It was Sophomore year now, and they did need him
sadly; for many of the giants who had won the championship the year before were gone.   But still Clarkson
refused to go into training, and the rest of the College,
at first puzzled by his conduct, gradually grew angry
and called him a coward, and a chump, and various
other uncomplimentary names.   Not to his face, to be
sure, for they still remembered that Freshman cane rush;
but in those evening gatherings where there are boys in
all the chairs and on the floor, where the air is blue with
tobacco smoke, and where all the problems of the uni-
verse are discussed and satisfactorily settled, from the
evolution of man to the best make of tennis racquet.

Finally, the new captain, who was a handsome young-
ster, with his blue eyes and fair cheeks, told the Professor's daughter all about it.   It has not been previously
remarked that Sam's professor possessed such a thing as
a daughter, but he did, and a very pretty one, too, as
any man in college could tell you.   She was a dainty
little thing, with dark hair that was forever straying in
bewitching locks and curls, and honest, deep grey eyes,
that she veiled coquettishly with long lashes.   As for the
tiny scarlet crescent of her mouth, it would tempt a
man to more than the steady curve of the rounded chin
would allow.

She was the only thing in the world of which Sam
would allow to himself that he was afraid.   He had
worshipped her with a sort of dumb longing since the
first time he had seen her.   One day he had driven her to
the railway station.   It was late autumn, and the chilly
air made her, unconsciously, perhaps, draw closer to

him. The faint perfume from her hair floated up into his face, and presently a wandering curl blew against his cheek. He could feel yet that electric thrill, and it was with a sense almost of danger that he had avoided her ever since.

But this day it had been impossible to elude her. She had met him squarely, and, her grey eyes flashing, she had said: "I did not expect *you*, Mr. Clarkson, to be a coward and disloyal to your college."

"Am I?" he asked quietly, but with a deep, dark flush on either cheek.

"Yes, you are," she replied. "You know our foot-ball team is weak and needs you badly—that Amherst is very likely to beat us. And still you refuse to play. I am very much disappointed in you, Mr. Clarkson."

"I am sorry," said Sam humbly, and stood aside for her to pass. Then he went to his little room and tried to work upon his Latin for the afternoon. But the lively verse of old Horace did not at all suit his frame of mind, and soon he found himself in a very black mood, hating himself and everyone else, but principally that handsome young captain, with his money and his wit and his walks with the professor's daughter.

Then he thought of her and the black changed to blue, and he was enjoying all the sombre delights of melancholy when there came a tiny tap at the door. He had only time for a hasty rub at his eyes before she entered. A little dab of powder under one eye looked as if she had been crying, too, but Sam did not notice that. He only knew that she was holding out both hands to him and saying:

"Will you forgive me for what I said, Mr. Clarkson? I wronged you cruelly, and I am very sorry. Father has just told me the truth."

There was a lump in Sam's throat that kept him from speaking, and she went on:

"But it is all right now. Father wants you to be his secretary, and he will pay you enough so that you will not need to do any other work, and will have plenty of time to play foot-ball. Will you?"

"Will I?" The tone of the voice answered the question.

Did he? Ask the left guard and centre on that season's Amherst team. I am sure they still remember how, not once or twice, but half a dozen times, in that season's championship game, there plunged between them a curly-haired young giant, whose onward rush was stopped only when the whole opposing eleven was clustered upon his shoulders like hounds upon an elk.

And I know that Clarkson and his wife still remember what the Professor's daughter cried: "Thirty-two to nothing! Oh, Sam! *Dear* Sam! It is glorious."

H. C. PEARSON, '93.

To the Connecticut River.

Low under the hills **where the shadows fly,**
  The pine trees **murmur,** the low winds sigh;
  And over the ripples of silver and shade
  The **moonlight streams like a pathway** laid.
  And the winds kiss **the leaves and the leaves** kiss the
      stream
  At the foot of the bank where I lie and dream.

  Your years will come and mine will go;
  You will continue **to** wind and flow;
    And into **your** depths the stars will fall'
    That **shine through** the tops of the hemlocks tall.
  And some other youth will **watch their gleam,**
  And lie at the foot of the **bank and dream.**

                         W. B. Plumer, '96.

THE CONNECTICUT.

"GAUDET TENTAMINE VIRTUS."

[The early chroniclers of Dartmouth remarked that the family device of the Earl of Dartmouth, "Gaudet Tentamine Virtus," seemed especially fitted to represent the spirit of the young College.]

YOU ask, my good friend, how it chances
   That Dartmouth men, where'er they stray,
Are nearing the front in life's battle,
And ne'er known to shrink from the fray.

Draw near, and I 'll tell you a story,
Though somewhat a secret, 'tis true,
Of Old World chivalrous glory
Forever maintained in the New.

Far o'er the sea lies an island,
The emerald gem of earth's zone,
Where Wit has perennial sources,
And Eloquence nurtures her own.

In the days of Erin's lost grandeur,
When her fingers so royally swept
Her golden harp-strings at Tara,
That for ages in sorrow have slept,

There flourished among her proud nobles
A chieftain of wisdom and might,
Whose crest was ever the foremost
In court, camp, council, or fight.

Now his was no usual sur-coat
That his arms emblazoned displayed,
On the moonlit shores of Killarney,
By the deft hand of fairies 't was made,

And his arms had a magical potence,
Conferred by their kindly behest,
Each loyal descendant's proud motto
Was: "Manhood delights in the test."

Years passed: o'er the hill-sides of granite
A Voice in the Wilderness cried,
And prompt in his generous succor
The staunch Earl of Dartmouth replied.

His birth made him the successor
To the power of the sur-coat, I ween,
And the crest that never was tarnished
Still ever the foremost was seen;

His name passed over the ocean
For the honored young college to bear,
And when green as its color was chosen
The magical charm was still there.

The earls of Dartmouth no longer
Grace the court or lend aid in the field,
But the enchanted device has grown stronger
In the might of our Dartmouth revealed;

And each man of our sterling old college,
In contest of brain or of brawn,
Inherits the motto's brave spirit
That urges him constantly on,

And, true to the crest of our patron,
He enters the conflicts of life
Endowed with the same Dartmouth feeling,
A manly delight in its **strife**.

W. F. GREGORY, '88.

AMONG THE HILLS.

*A*GAIN among the **hills**!
     The shaggy hills!
The clear arousing air comes like a call
Of bugle notes across the pine, and thrills
My heart as if a hero had just spoken.
     Again among the **hills**!
     The jubilant unbroken
     Long dreaming **of the** hills!

R. HOVEY, '85.

DARTMOUTH IN ENGLAND.

THE distinguished individual whose **portrait hangs in**
Wilson Hall was **the** Second Earl **of Dartmouth; the**
first Earl was created in **1711,** the first Baron **having
been** created in 1682; the arms **at that** time **being a
white** stag's head **on** an azure shield (dark green **would
have been more appropriate).** The crest was **five os-
trich feathers, alternating** blue and **white,** possibly **azure
and argent; underneath was a scroll, with** the motto,
"Gaudet tentamine virtus"; not entirely consistent with
that portion of the Lord's prayer which says "Lead us
not into temptation," and perhaps it will **not do to
encourage the employment of this** motto too strongly
among youths of tender **age,** who, **when they think they**
stand, should take heed **lest they fall.**

When the earldom was created **in** 1711, **there was**
added to the arms more imposing features — supporting
lions, with a ducal coronet in the crest, while the shield
was sown with fleur-de-lis and mullets.

The Dartmouth family name is Legge. Thomas Legge
was sheriff and Lord Mayor **of London in** the middle
of the fourteenth century; he loaned £300 **to Edward
III. to war with France, and therefore, I** suppose, came
into royal favor. His son William married Elizabeth,
daughter of Sir William Washington; **whether of the
Northumberland and** Durham Washingtons, **from whom**

Charles T. Gallagher, Hon. '93.

the father of our country, is claimed to have sprung, I am unable to say; but his son George commanded line-of-battle ships and was governor of Portsmouth, near Dartmouth, and he was made a peer, with the title of baron, in 1682.

The second baron was one of the Lord Justices, and was made Earl of Dartmouth and Viscount Lewisham in 1711, and *his* son, the second earl, was, as I understand it, the progenitor of the College.

There is little association, at present, between the town of Dartmouth and the present earl, who still lives in London; but the association of the Legge family of one or two centuries past was at Dartmouth, from which place many naval expeditions, particularly against the French, set out, and in these the family was interested, Dartmouth receiving its charter of municipality for having raised two ships for the service of the king, and later raised thirty-one ships and 757 men for subsequent wars against France.

So when Mr. Whittaker, with Rev. Samson Occum, the converted Indian, as an object lesson, went to England to raise funds which founded our College, the natural direction of Mr. Whittaker and Mr. Whitefield,—whom he met in London,—was to the Earl of Dartmouth, from whose section, in Old England, many hundreds of people had sailed to establish a New England in the new world; and thus it was that Lord Dartmouth allowed the use of his name and money in obtaining subscriptions throughout England for the establishment of a college, which started from Eleazer Wheelock's beginning; although, in some way, I have always given to

Mr. Thornton, the first treasurer, credit for a greater part of the success than to Lord Dartmouth.

The old town is one of which we may well be proud, either to have as an ancestor or to be its namesake; for, besides its beautifully picturesque location, it is one of the most interestingly historical places on the coast of England. It figures in Roman and Saxon history, and at the time when William the Conqueror parcelled out his kingdom among his followers, Dartmouth was of considerable importance. It is claimed that William Rufus left his hunting in Dartmoor forest, and embarked from here when he went to relieve the Castle of Mans in Normandy.

Chaucer says of his "Shipman": "For aught I know he was of Dertemouthe." Richard, the lion-hearted, sailed from here to the Holy Land with his crusaders, and many are the historical incidents claimed for the place, which time will not permit my relating.

It was the home of Hawkins and Sir Francis Drake; here Sir Walter Raleigh lived and smoked the first tobacco that he brought from North Carolina, while a rock in the river is pointed out where he was wont to regale himself with an afternoon pipe. His father-in-law, Sir Humphrey Gilbert, also sailed from Dartmouth on his voyages of discovery; Dartmouth, also, was the birthplace of Newcomen, who invented the steam engine, afterwards perfected by Watt.

The town is at the mouth of the Dart River, which takes its rise in Dartmoor, the highest point on the water shed, from which flow rivers north into the Bristol Channel, at points in the country of "Lorna

Doon " and Charles Kingsley's " Westward Ho "; while, to the south, the rivers flow, like the Dart, into the English Channel. The mouth of the river, about 150 yards in width, is flanked on either side by an ancient castle, restored and in a good state of preservation. Inside the mouth the river widens to a large harbor, capable of accommodating 500 vessels.

The local history states that Edward the Fourth made a bargain with the municipality of Dartmouth, in consideration of the payment of £30 annually forever, that they build and maintain, at the entrance of the harbor, "a stronge and mightye and defensyve new tower," with a boom and chain extending to the Castle at Kingswear on the opposite bank, an oil painting of which latter, by one of Dartmouth's students, hangs in the library building. The Dartmouth castle preserves its ancient appearance; but is occupied only by an ordnance sergeant of the British army, who has charge also of the fort adjoining, where the Devonshire artillery exercise the cannon in the casemates.

Adjoining the castle, also, is the ancient St. Petrox church, like the castle, built in the fifteenth century, and which also, like a portion of the castle, is partially covered with ivy. The two together make a most picturesque combination from every point of view, situated, as they are, on the rugged rocks at the mouth of the harbor, the green cliffs rising behind and beyond them, terminating in the higher lands, forming a most beautiful setting; above, on the river, extends the city of Dartmouth on the one side, and Kingswear, its companion, on the other, while between float vessels and boats, making of the whole a beautiful picture; up the stream, in the distance, lay those mammoth hulks of days gone by, the "Britannia" and "Hindoostan"— old three-deck line-of-battle ships, peacefully moored to furnish a school for naval cadets, conducted similar to our naval school at Annapolis; up the Dart river the scenery is most fascinating and beautiful, and is made one of the pleasure trips by people resorting to South Devon. Fifty years ago Her Majesty, the present Queen, wrote of it as reminding her of "the beautiful Rhine and its five castles and the Lorelei."

But one of the most important facts, and one which interests us more than anything else, outside of the association of the old town with the College, is the historical fact that practically from here sailed that little barque across "the mighty Western sea," freighted with a precious cargo that was to lay the corner-stone of a nation, the blessings of which we now enjoy; for the "Mayflower" and "Speedwell," after leaving Delfthaven, really sailed from Dartmouth as their last port of departure, and put into Plymouth only because the "Speedwell" was found unseaworthy, and her people were transferred to the "Mayflower" at that port; the "Mayflower," therefore, really made her passage from the town of Dartmouth, though she temporarily put into Plymouth for the above purpose. Therefore the town in New England, whose name has become associated with the strength and greatness of our nation, should be not Plymouth, but that given to our College, —Dartmouth.

C. T. GALLAGHER, HON. '93.

THE DARTMOUTH BUILDINGS ABOUT 1835.

THE DARTMOUTH BUILDINGS ABOUT 1835.

OUR second picture of the college knoll is from a colored lithograph made at Hartford, Conn., probably about 1830–1835. Already the general appearance was different enough from that of thirty years before.

The most conspicuous **change is** the presence of **the two** new dormitories, **then used exclusively** as such. **They** were named, **respectively, after** Governor Wentworth, and John **Thornton, of England, the** distinguished **benefactors of the college in its early struggles; al-**though, **for some time, they were spoken of colloquially as North and South** Halls. **Dartmouth Hall had** undergone within **a material renovation, including the crea-**tion of **the then new, but now "** Old " Chapel.

The foreground is rather fanciful, although the paths ran about as represented. The road shown just south of Thornton probably led merely **to the** rear of the Wheelock House, which, by the way, was then occupied **by a** Mrs. Carrington, who took boarders. The fences **would** seem to have been somewhat altered since **the** time of Mr. Ticknor's sketch.

The prosperity of **the** college was then increasing. **There were about 250 students, including about** 100 **medicals, though the faculty numbered only ten.** Some **of the customs and circumstances of that day** seem to **us a little strange. The college owned only the land on which these buildings stood; for not until late in the**

3

'40s, did it begin to acquire the rest of the Park square, and not for thirty years after that did it secure its present almost complete control. The necessary expenses were estimated in the catalogue at $101.22, including $27 for tuition, $3 for ordinary incidentals, and $54 for the 38 weeks' board. Commencement, originally celebrated in September, occurred then on the Wednesday preceding the last Wednesday of August. A vacation of four weeks followed, and there were others, of two and a half weeks in May and June, and of six and a half weeks, arranged for the large number who wished to teach, beginning in the latter part of January. Some years later this arrangement was altered. Attendance was made optional during an eleven weeks' winter term, when the chief part of the instruction was in the Modern Languages, which were considered rather unessential. Later yet, the convenience of the pedagogues was assured by great readiness on the part of the faculty to grant excuses for absence during the first weeks of the winter term. So a gradual evolution has gone on, until at present, since the work in the summer hotels has taken the place formerly held by teaching, the long summer vacation has come into being, and absence during the winter is paid for as dearly as at any other time.

R. H. FLETCHER, '96.

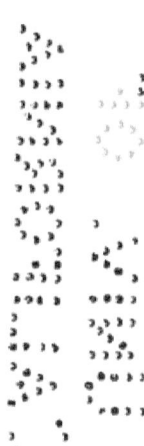

HARLAN COLBY PEARSON, '93.

.`

IN SENIOR DAYS. ,

HE little wood fire in the grate cast a narrow circle
of light into the enshrouding darkness. Within the
limits of its brilliance a daintily slippered foot and a
bit of silk stocking swung to and fro: while over opposite a pair of russet walking shoes were planted solidly
upon the polished floor.

From the direction of the slipper came a musical
voice, with a thoughtful note in it: "Charley, I've been
discussing the Sophoclean choruses with papa to-day.
And, Charley, do you really think they express the Greek
idea of a conscience, or what?"

The russet shoes suddenly withdrew from view, as if
their owner sat erect to reply: "My dear Florence, I'm
sure I don't know, and I hardly think I particularly
care. The way your respected father translates them,
they might express about anything."

The click of a button, and the soft glare of the electric
light illumined the becoming indignation of a very pretty
girl. "Charley — Mr. Dana — what do you mean? I did
not expect such a remark as that from you."

The dark-eyed young fellow in the great easy chair
smiled up at her a little impatiently, but, enjoying the
bright color in her cheeks, made no haste to reply: "Oh!
I beg pardon, of course. But we get so much of that

stuff over in Dartmouth, that one likes something else better from one's sweetheart, do n't you know."

"The proprietary air with which you say 'sweetheart,' Mr. Dana, is simply overpowering. But, if you regard an engagement as a prolonged billing and cooing, I must beg to be excused."

"Ah, yes! quite so. And if your fiancé must pass exams in Socrates and Sappho, I shall have to plug harder than I 've ever done yet."

The rose was changed to the lily now, and wrath made the brown eyes sparkle as brightly as the richly set solitaire that she threw in his lap. "It is evident, Mr. Dana, that I was very much mistaken in you a month ago. It is well we found it out so soon. Good evening!"

As she swept from the room with a queenly grace, Charley Dana watched her with an admiring smile. A smile that continued as he strolled under the broad-branching elms down the moonlit street; as he watched a glass marble and gaily-painted wheel revolve in opposite directions; and as, fifty dollars richer, he sank into a child-like sleep at 2 o'clock in the morning. For this was by no means his first "lovers' quarrel"; and he confidently relied upon his charms of face and manner to carry him through this, as they had the previous ones.

Whether or no Florence Huntley's pillow felt the touch of tears that night, is a lady's secret into which we will not pry. But the radiance of her smiles, next morning, fairly bewildered curly-haired little Teddy Bell. So completely was he overpowered, in fact, that the quality of his ball playing fell off perceptibly. Whereat the manager and captain held a long and serious consultation, for the final championship games were close at hand, and, with Teddy out of form, the chances of success were greatly diminished. But, as the fair Florence's favor continued, Teddy recovered all his old nerve, and felt that he could do better work than ever under the inspiration of her eyes.

That last Amherst game will never be forgotten by the men who saw it. The last half of the ninth inning, the score a tie, a Dartmouth man on third, and two hands out! From behind first and third bases, long, living, human lines converge. The cheering that was frantic a minute or two ago, grows mechanical, then ceases altogether. The nervous strain is terrible. A burly senior relieves himself by swearing, none too softly, and the grey-haired professor next him never thinks of reproof. Even the girls in the grand stand appreciate the crisis, and lean forward with breathless interest. Out in the field the auburn-crowned Amherst captain bites his lip till it bleeds, in his struggle to keep cool. Great drops of sweat stand out on the little pitcher's forehead, and his legs tremble in spite of himself.

The brown sphere shoots across the plate. "One strike," and Teddy Bell, bat at his shoulder, has moved not a muscle. "Two strikes," and a swelling, sullen murmur, like an angry sea, vibrates along the lines. The ball comes once more, swift and straight as an arrow. But this time it is met. Crack! and the spell is broken. A pretty hit, Mr. Stearns, just out of your reach. And the winning run is scored. Yell, Dartmouth, yell! Be madmen if you will. Forget that you are young or old, rich or poor, wise or foolish. Remember only that we have gloriously won a pennant. And you, Teddy Bell, **be proud as** you may, for this is the day of your exaltation. And lay away carefully, if you **will, the rose she** took from her breast to pin **on yours.**

*   *   *   *   *   *   *   *

Tuesday evening of Commencement week. **The glee club concert is over, and the** crowd, pouring out **of the** old gymnasium, turns its steps **up** the street **toward** Dartmouth hall. There the grey elms in the college yard have put forth their annual bloom of Chinese lanterns and electric bulbs; beneath them sounds the **pensive strain of** "After the Ball"; and around the distorted **circle of** the walks twists and curls an endless human **serpent.**

This young fellow in faultless evening **dress** chews his **moustache rather angrily.** And the trim little girl at his **side does not seem very** happy either; perhaps, because **she is manifestly his sister.**

"Charley," **she says, "you** never sang **better in your life. And you ought to be** proud of leading such **a glee club, too."**

"**Sure**," is the monosyllabic reply, whereat little **sister** looks up with mingled pity **and** vexation. Her face lights up a moment later, however, as an advancing **couple** are stopped and engaged in merry conversation.

Just how it happened no **one but** Kittie Dana **knew.** But when **the band struck** up another air she and Teddy Bell strolled away together, nursing a bad case of love **at first sight; and** Florence Huntley **and her former sweetheart were** left to their own devices.

I suppose they said a great deal to each other **in a very**

short time.   For it was not long before I saw them steal
"**far from** the madding crowd" up to the picturesque
solitude of Observatory hill.   And I alone know — prome-
nade concerts are guiltless of chaperones — what hap-
pened there, when, **as** the clock struck twelve, the
musicians packed up their instruments and the myriad
lights were extinguished.

How a shapeless monster in the little iron summer-
house dissolved into two parts.   And how, **before the**
separation took place, a smothered voice said:

"Charley, I just *hate* Greek choruses."

H. C. PEARSON, '93.

THE REASON WHY.

*A*S we sat, not a word passed between us —
    I'll tell you the reason why:
  We sat so close it would be no use
    For even a word to try.

J. W. BISHOP, '95.

THE OLD AND NEW.

THE old Year, the happy Year,
  The Year we used to know,
Stands shivering at the door tonight,
  And waits her turn to go.
We fain would clasp the pleading hands
  And smooth the wrinkled brow,
But Time has beckoned, and she says:
  "I must be going now!"

The new Year, the dawning Year,
  The Year that we shall know,
Comes romping in with baby feet
  From out the frost and snow.
She clambers high upon our knee,
  And whispers in our ear,
The while she clasps her chubby hands:
  "A Happy New Year!"

E. O. GROVER, '94.

EDWIN OSGOOD GROVER, '94.

A DARTMOUTH INVENTION.

IT is not, perhaps, generally known to present under-graduates that a Dartmouth catcher was the first to use the body-protector, which is now used by every catcher.

In the year of '82, the hopes of Dartmouth base-ball enthusiasts had been somewhat dampened by the announcement that the man best fitted for the position of catcher had been forbidden by his parents to play that position, for the catcher in those days was peculiarly liable to injury in the body, for which there was no protection.

So it was that the uninitiated were agreeably surprised to see their favorite catcher take his place behind the bat in one of the first Harvard games played that season.

Before many innings had been played, a swift foul tip had struck him full in the stomach, and the spectators leaned anxiously forward, expecting to see him doubled up with agony and carried from the field. What was their astonishment when they saw him instead, coolly pick up the ball and toss it to the pitcher. If this had happened among savages, the catcher would probably have gained some such name as "The Man with the Iron Stomach." As it was, the wonder of the observers was not lessened, until the matter was explained to them by the more intimate friends of the player, for, being much disappointed at his parents' refusal to let him catch, he had set his wits at work and devised a sort of padded cushion, which could be worn under his uniform, and did not in the least impede his **motions.** It was not very large, and fitted **so well that no** one would know from his appearance that he was thus protected.

From that time the protector became an essential **part** of every catcher's outfit.

Many **readers** of this will recognize **in the inventor one** of the most prominent of Dartmouth's **alumni.**

N. L. FOSTER, '96.

TO A WITHERED MAYFLOWER.

FAIR withered blossom, though thy tender leaves
    Are bruised and ragged torn,
  And thou, e'en of thy unassuming grace art shorn,
    Thou still art just as dear.

Undimmed the air thy fragrance yet receives.
    One breath so small,
Yet round me all
    The voices of thy piny home I hear.

F. V. BENNIS, '98.

Frederic Vucassovich Bennis, '98.

Sanborn Hall During the Reign of Terror of 1894-1895.

'TIS eight o'clock in Sanborn Hall; a placid quiet
　　reigns:
'Tis like the brewing of the storm that yet unseen
　　remains.
The Hall an air of wise research and classic study wears:
The only sounds are gentle steps which travel up the
　　stairs.

'Tis nine o'clock in Sanborn Hall; a murmuring sound is
　　heard;
The storm is gathering nearer now, but naught has yet
　　occurred:
A distant song comes from above and on our ears doth
　　fall,
But still a dignified repose hangs over Sanborn Hall.

'Tis half-past nine; the songs increase and float from
　　many bards;
From rooms near by, through open doors, we hear them
　　shuffling cards.
The money's chink, the glasses' clink, increase our anxious
　　fears,
As louder yet the rising sounds fall on our listening ears.

'Tis ten o'clock in Sanborn Hall; the sounds are now
    full loud;
In rooms above, in halls, on stairs, we hear the gather-
    ing crowd.
The time rolls on, the sounds increase, the noise becomes
    a din;
The joyous youths will now full soon their evening's
    work begin.

'Tis half-past ten; athletic games are played now, in the
    hall;
The racers rush, with clattering shoes, and oft-times
    loudly fall.
The bold contestants gather, then, and try, with all
    their might,
To see who first can hurl a ball against the electric light.

Eleven o'clock in Sanborn Hall; the lights are out and
    gone;
'Mid crashing sounds of splintering wood, we wish in
    vain for dawn:
A raging crowd attacks our door, which is not strong
    as rock;
They push and shove, they kick and slam, they try to
    pick the lock.

In wrath and dread we sit and swear, and watch our
    tottering door;
We prop it up with chairs and trunks, all piled upon the
    floor:

Some youths without have seized a trunk, and rush it
  up and down;
The noise is such we almost think 'twill wake the
  startled town.

Half-past eleven in Sanborn Hall; the noise is at its
  height;
A constant din from room and hall disturbs the calm of
  night:
The shutters, seized by ruthless hands, are dashed upon
  the ground,
But, 'mid the roar, we scarce can hear this slight and
  gentle sound.

'Tis twelve o'clock in Sanborn Hall; the crisis now is
  o'er:
Though still the din is wild and fierce, 'tis less than 'twas
  before.
A few, who dread tomorrow's sun, are hastening from
  the Hall;
Their echoing footsteps, as they go, shake ceiling, floor,
  and wall.

'Tis twelve-fifteen in Sanborn Hall; our door is left, at
  last;
The crowd decides to haste to bed; the sounds grow
  gentler fast.
"Good-night! Good-night!" we hear the call; and then,
  oh, sad to tell,
The answer to this kindly wish is simply, "Go to ——!"

'Tis half-past twelve in Sanborn Hall; the sounds are
    growing low:
The crowd has thinned, and those who stay prepare to
    bed to go;
My friend and I, with weary sigh, prepare to go there too,
A thing which, for the last two hours, we much have
    wished to do.

   *   *   *   *   *   *   *   *

'Tis eight o'clock in Sanborn Hall; the day is bright and
    hot:
The janitor arrives and sees, and cries, in woe, "GREAT
    SCOTT!"
He meets the leader of the band, who, sauntering down
    the hall,
Remarks, "They made such noise last night I could not
    sleep at all.

"A band of 'medics' came, you know, and made a devil-
    ish row;
I tried to study up my 'trig.,' but I don't know it now.
I wish those 'blamed,' confounded fools would keep out
    in the street";
And then he goes off to his club, and sits him down to eat.

   *   *   *   *   *   *   *   *

'Twas thus it was in Sanborn Hall, in days that now
    are gone;
'Twas thus the revellers raged and slammed from eve far
    on towards dawn.
We cannot pierce the future's veil, or see what will befall;
We *hope* that now a peaceful calm will reign in Sanborn
    Hall.   C. N. McCALL, '98.

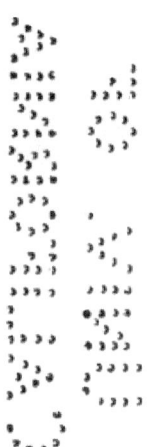

HARRIE SHERIDAN BAKETEL, D. M. C.

OUT WITH THE TIDE.

IT had been an awful night. For **hours the wind had howled and** moaned about this tiny cottage nestled **among** the cliffs. Now it resembled the awful roar **of a lion, and now the soft** and plaintive wailings of an **infant. The storm had** spent its fury, but the waves still **beat upon the rocky shore,** with that **sullen roar** which **portends** approaching evil.

"Old man, the tide is going out." As if from the sep-**ulchre** came those words, and they brought a chill of **terror** to the person addressed. "Jack, it is near the **ebb.** Draw closer: I wish to talk with you." Again came that sepulchral voice, and once more the hearer started.

In one corner of the room, reclining upon a rough bed, lay **the prostrate form of a man** of thirty, a man whose wasted **face bore traces of aristocratic breeding** and **former good looks. In** height he stood perhaps six feet, **with a body built in proportion.** His shapely head was **covered** with a luxuriant growth of straight black hair, while a heavy mustache hid a set of pearly teeth. His **face bore a most determined air, in spite of** the ravages of illness, and great strength of character was clearly portrayed there. The sick man possessed the general air of a gentleman, although he was in a fisherman's hut.

The person addressed was of an entirely different type. A short stature, a grizzled countenance, almost amounting to a frown, and deep-set, piercing eyes, characterized Jack Amazeen, the fisherman. He had long passed the half-century milestone, but looked as rugged as the cliffs he loved so well.

Almost a year before, after a great storm, a boat was washed ashore, in which was found the apparently lifeless body of a man. The ever-generous Amazeen took the storm-tossed stranger to his humble cottage, and there nursed him back to life. This man, cast up by the sea, gave the name of Jackson — Thomas Lee Jackson — but more than that no one knew. He never mentioned his antecedents nor anything of his past life. His rough associates, thinking he had some trouble on his mind, did not press the subject, and soon he became with the rest — in body, if not in spirit — a common fisherman.

Time passed on. The new-comer, evidently accustomed to luxury, could not stand the hardships of such a life, and was stricken down with fever. With the winter his illness increased, until on this cold, wild night the climax had come. "Jack, it is near the ebb. Draw closer: I wish to speak with you." Amazeen did as he was bid. With a touch almost as gentle as a woman's, he smoothed out the pillows and changed to a more comfortable position the weary sufferer.

"Jack," he began, "I have never told you of my life, but I feel the end approaching, and I wish to die in

peace. Far away in a little Virginia town, surrounded
by beautiful trees and well-kept lawns, is situated the
manor house of Thomas Lee Jackson, my father. There,
in that house, quite thirty years ago, I was born, and
there for eighteen years I lived, as happy and innocent
as a boy could be. I had seen nothing of the world,
its trials and troubles, and knew only happiness. My
mother was a proud, high-spirited, yet lovable woman,
and to her I owe my gentleness of disposition. My sire
was of an old and highly aristocratic family. He had a
cold and stern manner, which made me respect him, but
killed all thoughts of love. My constant playmate
was a black-eyed, dark-haired little maiden, by name
Helen La Fetra. Her family came originally from
New Orleans, and she possessed all the traits of a
Creole. When very young our mothers decided we
should marry when the proper time came, and we grew
up with no other thought. I believed I loved Helen.
She was a beautiful girl in feature and character, and
her only fault was the presence of the green-eyed monster, jealousy.

"Shortly after my eighteenth birthday it was decided
I should enter the St. Thomas's School for Boys, situated within a few minutes' ride of Philadelphia. Naturally I was greatly pleased with the prospect, and im-
mediately informed Helen as to my future plans. She
cried and mourned so that my heart was touched, and I
allowed that I would stay at home. But *père* Jackson
listened to no such childish excuse, and in a few days I
had bade my betrothed farewell. For a few months all
was pleasant. Frequent and tender missives found their

4

way between St. Thomas's School and that little Virginia town, and Helen and I were happy.

"Suddenly there came a change. One afternoon, while walking down Chestnut street in Philadelphia, I met my fate. Hers was the most divine face I had ever seen. It seemed to my boyish nature that she must be an angel on earth, and yet I had never heard her voice. That face haunted me by day, and was in my dreams at night. For weeks I spent my leisure hours in wandering up and down the streets of that city, longing for a glimpse of *la belle inconnue*. At length my hopes were realized. One day, in company with two fellow-students, I entered a large store, and the first person I beheld was she. My ideal a shop-girl! I quailed at the thought, but, student-like, found a pretext to speak.

"That visit was but the first of many. I need not tell how I met her when work was over and escorted her to the neat, yet cheerless apartments where she lived with an invalid mother and younger sister; how I partook of their simple meals, read with her, sang with her, and sped the hours in the thousand ways known to lovers. Ah, Jack, those were happy days! I met her as a boy, but those experiences transformed me into a man.

"My father! How faint I grew when I imagined myself before him, venturing the information that I loved a shop-girl! And Helen—she to whom I was affianced! Recklessly I went on, falling deeper and deeper in love with Susie—her name was Susie Winsted—until she became a part of my very life.

"The summer came, and with it the time for my departure. I will say nothing of my leaving: it is too sacred. From the time I met Susie my letters to Helen had been irregular, but she received me as if constancy had been personified. I dreaded to tell my father, for I knew the inevitable result; yet it remained undone, and I resolved to take courage. The result was worse than I anticipated. He raved and swore, and declared that I should marry Helen or leave his house forever. Despite the vain entreaties of my mother his will was firm. Give up Susie? Never! I would sooner have sold my chances of heaven.

"But my meeting with Helen—how can I ever describe it? Ah, plainly do I see her now, though eleven years have passed since that day. She stood in the drawing-room, dressed in a loose, flowing white gown, with red rosebuds at the throat, and a diamond-crested dagger in her hair. She was no longer the lovable girl I had loved, indeed, a fiend had taken that place. And the words she spoke!—a little water, please, old man; yes, I feel better now—Oh, God! what words! She brought down the curses of a thousand devils upon me and mine forever. Glad was I when she fainted, permitting me to leave. I went home and craved my father's pardon. It was useless: he was immovable.

"A few months found me in Philadelphia, clerking in a store, married to my love. For a while nothing marred our happiness, and I had almost forgotten Helen's curse, but such happiness could not endure. Susie was about to realize the fondest anticipations of a woman's heart.

"Her invalid mother was seriously injured by a fall and died in a short time. The shock was too great for my girl-wife. She was stricken down, and the end came sooner than I expected. All night long the doctors watched over and administered to her, but as the tide went out, the spirit of all that was dear to me was swept out upon the great unknown sea, and with it went the soul of our little boy. The curse! the curse! How little did I think it would come to that!

"Then my life became a blank. I shipped as a sailor, thinking death might come sooner, but fortune had decreed otherwise. We were wrecked, but the curse was over me, and I was washed ashore. You know the rest. Jack, when I am gone I want you to write to my father and tell him of my end, and—just one more sip of water. Let me sleep a little while, and I'll tell you the rest." The wanderer turned on his couch, and soon was wrapped in a peaceful slumber.

The dawn was fast approaching, and the tide was going out. The wind died away. The ocean roared as before. The sick man slept on. His dreams seemed disturbed, and incoherent mutterings intermingled with his breathing. The sun rose above the great hills far off to the eastward, and the dull gray faded as its bright rays crept above the horizon. A single ray of light stole in through the little window, playing about the sufferer's face. It brightened up the care-worn features as with a light from heaven. The man awoke with a ghastly fire burning in his eyes, but a seraphic smile lighted up his countenance.

"Jack, my boy, the tide has nearly ebbed. Listen, do you hear that music, the sound of voices, and, Jack, look yonder, I see the river and angels on the other side, and oh, Jack! there — in — the — midst — is — Susie — my —

Susie "—and with hands outstretched, and the name of his beloved on his lips, the noble spirit of Tom Jackson left its earthly frame.

The tide had ebbed. The wind moaned a solemn requiem, and the waves, as they beat against the rocky cliffs, sang a farewell mass for the departed soul.

H. S. BAKETEL, D. M. C.

RENEWAL.

I SAW one faring up the hills of Life
 　Beneath a sultry noon-tide's blazing beams;
His shield bore dents from many a field of strife,
His rusty mail was gashed in gaping seams.
He walked alone, a pilgrim staff for spear,
Nor called for help, believing none would hear.

I saw him once again far up the height;
Upon his staff a pennon fair unfurled,
His peerless brow was radiant with light,
He moved in strength with thews to throw the world.
Before the victor fled his foeman grim,
For he was mighty since Love walked with him.

O. S. DAVIS, '89.

The Campus.

WHERE once the pine tree tossed its lordly head,
   Where once the Indian spread his hemlock bed,
Where hooting owl his portent shrilly screamed,
And eyes of crouching panthers glowed and gleamed;
'Tis there it spreads its bosom to the sky,
Reflects the clouds that bending o'er it lie
To look where year on year they see again
The groups of happy youths and learned men.

'Tis long since hardy hands the axe raised high,
And felled those haughty gazers at the sky.
'Tis long since noble Wheelock's kindly voice
Directed those who made of wisdom choice.
Full eighteen whites, six Indians he brought;
'Mid heavy works and trials these he taught
To read, to write, but best to be a man;
They lived in humble ways: a saw-mill ran.

A thousand snows have on thy bosom lain,
A thousand suns have burned them off again,
And here, where once a forest vast was seen
Expands beneath the stars our college green.
The hush of night a lonely air distils,
But happiness my soul awakes and thrills,
As falls the moonlight on our elm-edged ground
Where manly hearts are e'er united found.

Fletcher Harper Swift, '98.

Brave Wheelock, Webster, Choate, and many more
Have trod, as I do now, this shining floor.
They hourly come in all their strength to mind;
Departing, leave their presence yet behind.
How many feet have trod this glist'ning plain,
How many here will never come again :
Then let us strive to be as they were then,
And, striving, be what Dartmouth knows as MEN.

F. H. SWIFT, '98.

THE STUDENT'S VISION.

H E sleeps; no care
    Is in his youthful mind,
And softly through his wavy hair
    The early morning sunbeams wind,
And weave a halo, such as masters old
Have limned above the virgin's hair of gold.

He sleeps; 'mid dreams
    There breaks a sudden sound,
And shivering, to him it seems
    A hundred demons howl around.
And as he tries to break the awful spell
He wakes; he groans — it is the chapel bell.

F. H. NOYES, '97.

AFTER SUNSET.

HANOVER has two exteriors each year, as distinct as the two coats of a rabbit. There is the long event introduced by the terror-bringing call for foot-ball, and ushered out by the whirl of Commencement; and then follows that calm, lonely, beautiful time of the summer vacation. The student who knows only the first, never has gained a half conception of the college town. He must come back when the crickets are first beginning to rasp out their mournful monotones from the grass-tufts, and mope for an evening on the steps of Dartmouth Hall, before he can claim to be closely acquainted with Hanover. There is just enough mist clinging half-perceptibly to the campus, just enough after-glow in the west, just enough of a threat of the full moon in the east, to invite one's recollection to wander; and thus, all through the hush of the evening, while the day's sounds are giving place to those of the night, the alumnus on the stone steps hears voices to which other ears are deaf, and sees sights which fail the few who are abroad. Long, weird cries again rouse the energy of the Freshmen, gathering near the "Gym" with something mysterious tucked away under the coat of a leader. Under the windows again sounds the "Oh-h Jack!"—that strange call, with the prolonged and mellow droning of the "oh," and the rifle-like explosion of the

"Jack." · A grand-stand and a crowd, too; **a tumult of** lusty shouting, and then a long suspense; one **last yell,** one mass of surging men,—and then the bell and **horns.** Through the shadows a solitary form rushes along **the** sidewalk, while the bell above tolls dismally; his **pace increases,** the bell never falters, and he disappears under the low arch just as the bell strikes its doleful double-stroke. This was one of the **men** who "sleeps o'nights." And then **a** long line of **figures keeps steady pace over** that same walk. They **enter the door.** Finally **the notes** of "Amesbury" come floating **out:**

> "Our life is a dream,
> Our time as a stream
> Glides swiftly away."

And once, before the dampness **drives the** careless alum-**nus to** his close room, there passes before him the face and figure of Ned—Ned, the fellow whom **few of the** men liked. The faculty **said he wasn't strong.** But he had a heart **in** him **as kind as the heart of a mother.** And they laid **him** away **in a** narrow house of earth, the other day, the first one **of the** class **to go;—so,** perhaps, the fact that there was something like **a lump** of lead in the old graduate's throat as he walked away, will be thought no weakness,—for, **after all, though few can reason,** all can feel; and this **common lot of pain and loss** makes us all **close** kindred **in the long run. Yes,** indeed, there are two phases to the college town among the hills! Happy and **sad are** those who can live over by memory the tumult **of** one amid the repose of the other.

O. S. DAVIS, '89.

THETFORD SKETCHES.

WIDOW JOHNSON, who was postmistress in the little village, was unusually long in distributing the small pile of mail that had just come in from the south. The seven or eight farmers who crowded the "office," were discussing loudly the relative weight of two pair of oxen, and vainly trying to decide how much corn had "riz sence 'lection." In one corner of the room, and watching the open fire, sat a young girl, perhaps eighteen, though she appeared much younger. At last all of the papers were distributed among the twenty-five or thirty boxes which composed the post-office, and Widow Johnson exclaimed:

"Well, that's the biggest mail I've had yet. One could tell it was nigh Christmas. There was seventeen letters, and most as many papers. No, Deacon Thompson, your *Hanover Gazette* didn't come. It's queer, isn't it?"

"Wa'al, 't is queer," said Deacon Thompson, as he stroked his long, white beard; "it hain't missed afore for nigh onto a year. And just when I want to know the news, too. I hear that Charlie Green has sold that cow of his."

Just then, Tilda Higgins, who had been quietly waiting her turn by the fireplace, came up, and Widow Johnson said, as she handed Tilda her father's *Gazette* and a postal, "That's one of them big postal cards from Joe

FALLS OF THE CONNECTICUT.

Brown in Dartmouth. Joe says that he's coming up to spend Christmas. 'Spose you are glad, Tilda?"

Tilda did not answer, but blushed profusely as she read the postal which Widow Johnson had just "glanced at," as she said, "to see if any one was dead." Joe Brown's father's farm was next to the Higgins's, and Joe and Tilda had made mud pies together, and had had the measles at the same time. But now Joe was in Dartmouth college, and every one in the little village looked up to Joe as the embodiment of all that was great. To be sure, Joe was only a freshman, but, to Tilda, and, in fact, to all, freshman and senior were alike. Of course, it was only a friendship that existed between Joe and Tilda, still Tilda couldn't help blushing whenever any one mentioned Joe in her presence.

*   *   *   *   *   *   *   *

It was the next day after Christmas. It had been bleak and cold, and Joe had spent his time in telling his father and mother strange stories of college life, and in eating apples.

Just before dark Tilda's little brother Sam was seen coming " 'cross lots." Joe met him at the door with, "Hullo! Sammy; how's Tilda?" "Oh, Tilda's all right," said Sam, "and she says as how she wants to have you come over and pop corn tonight. You'll come?"

"Of course I'll come, if Tilda wants me to," replied Joe.

Early that evening Joe took the well-worn path across

the fields to Tilda's. As he passed the window he saw Tilda sitting with her mother, sewing.

"Hullo! Joe," said Tilda, as he came in, "I'm so glad you came, 'cause it's terribly lonesome these long evenings."

"Darning stockings, I see," replied Joe, as he took up Tilda's work.

"Why, Joe," said Tilda, "that's one of those society panels that you asked me to make for you. Don't you think it's pretty? Tell us about how you joined that funny-named society. Do they really have a goat, and did they brand you, Joe?"

Joe then told Tilda all about college and the college town. How near he came to getting lost the first day, and finally about his initiation into the Pi Kappa Pi society. It was nine o'clock before they knew it, and no corn was popped. Mr. and Mrs. Higgins and Sammy all retired, and left Joe and Tilda to pop their corn together.

They sat in perfect silence for a few minutes, till the snapping of the corn in the popper sounded louder than the beating of Joe's heart. At length, as Joe filled the popper again, he began to talk ramblingly about the weather, his chum in college, and a girl he met last summer. Evidently Joe was uneasy. He had known Tilda a long time, and she knew it. But did she know that a freshman was supposed to be engaged to *some one?* When Joe had led the conversation up to the right point, and the corn-popping was at its height, he said, nervously, "Say, Tilda, it's strange, isn't it, how corn pops? I wonder how they do it?"

" Why, they just pop," replied Tilda.

Joe's heart failed him at this seeming rebuff, but he was soon ready for another attempt. "We have known each other a long time, haven't we, Tilda ?" said he.

"We have, that's a fact," answered Tilda, "but **I've** known Tom Wiggins longer."

Tilda did not seem to realize, in the least, that Joe was trying to discover **the way** the corn **popped,** and always answered with some commonplace remark his most pointed questions. Finally **Joe burst out** with, "Tilda, I want to tell you something before I go **about** "—

"**Oh, do**n't bother, Joe; you can tell me all about that foot-ball rush tomorrow night, when we have lots of time; let's just *talk* **now.**"

Joe was unusually cool when he said good-night soon **after,** and only remarked, as they stood in the door-**way,** that he should have **to** return to college the next **morning.**

*   *   *   *   *   *   *   *

At **ten o'clock,** the next morning, **the twelve by** fifteen station was **well** filled with passengers waiting **for** the **down train, which** was due at 10.15. **Mr.** Higgins was there with a box of butter to ship, and Widow Johnson had just run over from the post-office to bring her basket of eggs, which she sent **off** each morning. Joe Brown was alone with his thoughts and his small trunk, and was feeling very lonesome after the failure of the evening before. He had just dropped a penny in the slot of one of those weighing machines, and was about **to step on,** when he **saw** Tilda coming down the road toward the station. Here is another chance, thought he, and, forgetting all about his weight, he walked out to meet her. He had only three minutes to do it in, but he would make another try. By the time they had reached the station again the train had drawn in. As they walked toward the rear platform, Joe said, in a trembling voice, "Come, Tilda, you know what I was driving at last night while we were popping corn. I was trying to pop-pop the question. Can't we be engaged?"

"Why, of course, Joe," answered Tilda. "I wondered, last evening, why you didn't speak of it. Father won't know anything about it; he's loading his butter into the car. It's just lovely, isn't it? Good-bye."

"Good-bye."

E. O. GROVER, '94.

FROM THE RUINS OF THE OLD PINE.

O MATER, more than loved of me,
  Who from its planting watched this tree;
  The mighty pine may prostrate lie,
  May bow its aged head and die, —
The years have only youth for thee.

F. L. PATTEE, '87.

FRED LEWIS PATTEE, '88.

Mount Desert from the Sea.

O ROUGH, rude, rugged range of hills,
   Uprising from the sea!
With long forgotten rapture thrills
   My heart at sight of thee.

On old Green Mountain's rocky crown
   Would I could stand again,
And gaze the waters up and down
   That lave the feet of Maine—

Once more could climb up Newport's side,
   From care and trouble free,
And watch the gallant war-ships ride,
   Columbia's argosy.

Within thy virgin woods and bowers,
   O, fair Mount Desert isle,
I'd pluck again thy choicest flowers,
   And bask in Nature's smile.

Farewell, sweet isle, thy shores recede
   From my reluctant gaze.
Though I must leave thee, thou would'st lead
   Me back to happy days.

                A. O. Caswell, '93.

THE OLD PINE.

BRAVE old Pine, the swiftly passing years
 Have hushed the music of the sweet refrain
That breathed thy whispering boughs.   It is in vain
We sadly mourn thy death.   Thou hast no peers
To claim our love, and memory reveres,
And in her inmost shrine will e'er retain
The imprint of thy life.   May we attain
The grandeur in our lives of thy long years.
Thy dark, green boughs festooned with whirling
        throngs
Of snow-flakes soft, a robe of beauty wore,
And Dartmouth chose the glorious green and white.
The echo of a hundred parting songs
Thy branches flung.   With hearts too full for more,
Old Pine, we leave thee with one last "Good-bye.".

                    LE. B. M. HUNTINGTON, '98.

THE DARTMOUTH BUILDINGS IN 1851.

THE DARTMOUTH BUILDINGS IN 1851.

IT is **an** unsettled question whether **or not the** quality of a person's work is necessarily **affected by** his moral character. **The evidence** of the accompanying picture **seems to** be in **the** negative; for, while **it is** indisputably superior to that of Mr. Ticknor, it **was engraved —** in **1851**, from **a** daguerreotype — by a famous counterfeiter, **C.** Meadows, better known as "Bristol Bill," **then serving** a sentence in Windsor jail.

The principal change in the yard, since the time of the **preceding** view, had been the erection of Reed Hall. The second story of this building **was** occupied **by the** libraries of the college and the two societies, the United Fraternity and the Social Friends, which, together, **at the** time of its construction, numbered only about **fifteen** thousand volumes. These libraries were entirely separate until 1874, and **were not united on the shelves for** five years after that.

Thornton and Wentworth **Halls** appear here — more accurately than in the lithograph — as unpainted. They were first **washed** yellow about 1869, as was Reed at **the time of** its construction; **a** better taste has since **given all three more suitable tints.** Dartmouth, apparently, was always **white until about 1865.**

The representation **of the** yard appears accurate. **The**

5

fence, evidently, had been again changed. The road beside Wentworth remained until the building of Rollins Chapel rendered desirable its removal a few rods northward. The tree conspicuous in the foreground is the "Webster Elm," even then giving promise of its present magnificence. As the picture partly indicates, at this time the rain had hollowed out the heart from the junction of the limbs, and made for itself on one side a place of egress. Somewhat later, Prof. Blaisdel and Prof. Hubbard filled the whole cavity with brick and mortar.

The common, here first appearing, has, of course, an interesting history. Over it — where now is the present main path — ran for years the old turnpike. Its ownership was, almost from the beginning, a matter of dispute between the town and college. Among other things, the villagers long claimed and exercised the right to pasture there their cows. This custom the students bitterly resented, — although, as late as 1820, some of their own number were accustomed to keep those useful animals — and very often, about Commencement time, the Freshmen and Sophomores would drive away the whole herd, sometimes to a spot three or four miles distant, sometimes even to the basement of Dartmouth Hall. At last, in 1835, the disputed territory was levelled, planted with potatoes, and surrounded by a temporary fence. This latter the dissatisfied among the townspeople tore down, but the next year certain individuals of the faculty and town clubbed together and erected a permanent one. That summer the Common served for a grain field, but ever since it has been devoted to sports, and, until the present athletic field was prepared, in 1893, it was the regular college base-ball and foot-ball ground.

It was at just about this time,—in 1852,—that the second of the associated departments, the Chandler School, was established, by a bequest from Abiel Chandler, of Walpole, N. H. In the second "academy" building it continued a separate existence until its consolidation with the academical department in 1893.

R. H. FLETCHER, '96.

THE WAY IT FEELS.

I.

IT makes a fellow blue
        To flunk!
I thought I'd rush him, too,
        Then flunk!
But now I'll stop this play,
And buckle down and say,
I'll rush him ev'ry day;
        Not flunk!

II.

I'm happy as they come,
        A rush!
I'm not a little glum,
        A rush!
Could read the thing at sight,
The one I plugged last night.
It makes you feel 'bout right,
        To rush!

G. A. GREEN, '98.

Pastels in Prose.

In the Park at Midnight.

The ragged remnant of the Old Pine gazes tenderly at me through the nocturnal light:

Like a huge sentinel wrapt in his gray mantle the tower stands guard upon the hill-top. With its dark moon-shadow, which rests upon the grass-grown rocks, it reaches out to the darker shadows of the evergreens.

Arm-in-arm in each other's shade, the trees stand restful and asleep in the silence.

You can hear their gentle breathing as the breezes play among their tasseled tops.

The ragged remnant of the Old Pine gazes tenderly at me through the nocturnal light:

Like skeletons of former ghosts the summer houses are raised indistinct against the orient sky.

Winding snake-like among the shadows of the mingled leafage, the graveled walks run smooth and still.

With open arms the Bema embraces the lingering moonlight, and reveals its grassy plot of ground in the darkness of its overhanging rocks.

Hiding, as it were, in its own shadow, the Grotto peers out into the mellow moonlight. Only the grim blackness of its own visage is visible in its rocky cavern.

The ragged remnant of the Old Pine gazes tenderly at
me through the nocturnal light :

But a beauty not born of color dwells in this solitude.
A beauty in black. A blending of moonlight and
shade, that makes the meanest object lovely. A half in-
distinctness, which lends a grandeur to the towers of the
chapel and the church, as they rise into the low light of
the moon above the campus.

The surrounding hills are felt only by the oppressive
blackness of their invisible forms. We can see the ferns
and grasses fan with gentle breath the unopened blossoms of tomorrow at our feet.

But, hark! The old clock in the gilded dome of Dartmouth Hall is telling in sounding numbers Time's midnight beads.

The ragged remnant of the Old Pine gazes tenderly at
me through the nocturnal light :

E. O. GROVER, '94.

FAREWELL.

O DARTMOUTH HALL, that, gravely smiling,
    Gav'st us thy welcome years ago,
And watched us, drowsy hours beguiling,
    Stretched on thy grassy lawn below;
We pray of thee a parting blessing,
    Our first, our firmest college friend, —
We come, a thousand faults confessing,
    To crave thy pardon at the end.

And thou, O Pine, of Dartmouth's story
    The type, in thy rough majesty,
Here, in the evening's dying glory,
    We bid a last farewell to thee.
With solemn care, yet ever tender,
    Thou gazest on the student throng;
Our guardian, to thee we render
    The parting tribute of our song.

Ye, too, O hills and vales, now lying
    Half in the shadow, half in sun,
We say farewell to you, half sighing,
    And yet half glad that all is done.
For joy is mingling with the sorrow, —
    To learn was not the whole of life;
We greet a freer, stronger morrow,
    A morrow rich in earnest strife.

                                K. KNOWLTON, '94.

Kent Knowlton, '94.

WITH THE DAWNING.

THE hanging lamp, exhausted by its long night's vigil, gleamed fitfully through its rose-colored shade. Around the heavy draperies at the windows the pale light of early dawn stole in sufficiently to reveal the disorder of the room. Half-burned cigarettes, and cards, thrown down impatiently in the heat of play, strewed the floor. A heap of empty bottles in one corner matched the overflowing box of ivory chips upon the centre-table, around which were grouped significantly a quartette of empty chairs. On the low, broad sofa, his ulster thrown carelessly about him, a curly-haired boy was sleeping heavily.

From his perch on the cushioned window-seat Dick Ernst regarded the scene with manifest disfavor. The condition of the room was, in fact, in striking contrast to that of its owner, who, outwardly, showed scarcely a trace of the night's dissipation. From his dark, rich smoking jacket to his neatly slippered feet he was quite as nattily presentable as when, early the previous evening, he had met the president's daughter on the street and strolled home with her, the envy and admiration of many an under-classman. Even his handsome, boyish face appeared none the worse for the sleepless hours spent, save for the dark shadows just beneath his brown eyes.

But, however fresh and vigorous he might seem, Dick

was compelled to acknowledge **to himself** that he felt
like a wreck. "He lives a week in a day," some of his
friends had said of him, and the results were rapidly becoming manifest to himself, if not to others. His head
felt as if a giant hand was grasping it, as in a vise,
while dwarfish demons ran red-hot needles **through** his
temples. The lassitude, that comes with long-continued
loss of sleep, made him lie back wearily upon the cush-
ions, and his hand trembled so that he could hardly fill
his meerschaum from the china jar at his side.

He was not inclined to sleep, **so,** scarcely knowing
what to do, he drifted into thinking of himself and his
college course. Almost four years ago he had come to
Stonehenge **with** plenty of money and **a** good fit.
Brought up in isolation, however, by an eccentric uncle,
he knew **as little** of **the** living, rushing world, as the
wiry pony he rode about the **ranch.** In his first year at
college he had surprised his instructors by the steady ex-
cellence, and occasional brilliancy **of his work, while, out
on** the campus, his mates had learned to respect **his**
agility, strength, and ready adaptability.

But increasing popularity brought increased tempta-
tions. Just a glass of beer with the boys had led, by
senior year, to the best stocked corner cupboard in college, while the mildly exciting penny-ante had grown
into a game that had made No. 21 long a favorite scene
for *sub rosa* stories. In all the **county round, too,**
Dick 's **more** or less shady exploits had made his **name** as
familiar as the college president 's. And now, on this
wintry morning of his senior **year**, it was not a bright
picture that he looked **back** upon, but a dreary vista of

wasted opportunities, worse than wasted talents, days, months, and years of vicious idling. An aching head, an empty pocket, the boon companionship of rascals and good-for-nothings, these were the results.

He thought of the men who had just left him, and reviled himself for descending to their level. De Forest Davidson, christened Patrick Leary, proprietor of Davison's Daisies, at the opera house for one week, had been ushered in by his new-made friend, Tom Glynn, the hotel clerk. "Just to make up the game," Starr, the law student, had slipped in; a pale-faced youth, whose past record was as doubtfully suggestive as his handling of the cards. Ernst was naturally dainty and fastidious, if not pure and moral, and the constant oaths and vile jests of these vagabonds disgusted him even in remembrance.

"Anyway," he said, half defiantly, "I've harmed only myself. It's no one's business."

The sleeping boy on the sofa sat upright. "Full to aces," he cried, triumphantly. "What, four deuces?" And he sank back with a groan to his restless slumbers. The troubled look in Dick Ernst's eyes grew darker. Since entering Stonehenge the year before, "Little Brandon," thrown in his way by chance, had followed in his footsteps, copying his words, deeds, and even appearance, so far as he was able. Dick, on his side, petted the boy in a careless way, and, unthinkingly, gave him a flying start toward the goal of ruin.

He had spent the last vacation with the Brandons at their Sorrento summer home; and there he had met Her. Every incident of those happy days came back to him as he gazed across the room at the sleeping boy. She had avoided him at first, with the instinctive dislike a pure woman always feels towards a roué. But his winning charm, so potent when he chose, soon made her dream of influencing his life for the better; and then the result was inevitable. The night before he left he had told her the old, old story, amid the thundering of the surf, and she had listened with a blush and smile of happiness that, for a moment, drove every baser impulse from his nature.

He cursed himself for his folly now, as he thought of his neglect of her of late, and of the evil influence he had exerted over the brother she loved. Impulsively he strode to the window and pulled back the heavy hangings. The morning sun, grown rosy, warm, and bright, flooded the room with its brilliancy. It illumined Her picture on the opposite wall, and gave the clean, delicious face the tinge of life. Dick, exhausted and unnerved, imagined that her eyes followed him everywhere about the room, with a look half sorrowful, half reproachful, but wholly loving.

Suddenly the bonds that his pride and vice had drawn around him were burst by his passion. He fell on his knees before the picture, and, with his head buried in his hands, prayed Her God for forgiveness and for help. Little Brandon, awakened by the brilliant light, opened his eyes in astonishment at the scene. Then he turned toward the wall and wept, so quietly that Dick never knew.

So a new and sweeter chapter in two life stories began with the dawning.

H. C. PEARSON, '93.

WILDER DWIGHT QUINT, '87.

To an Honored Cane.

THOU portly stick of genial yellow,
  Full many a pave thou'st trod with me;
 Staunch to thy hickory core, old fellow,
  Friend from the days that used to be.

Under the elms of our Mother royal
  Four score of knives thy shell did hack.
 Thou touched the hands of a phalanx loyal,
  For "Simp," and "Biler," and "Doc," and "Quack,"

And "Sam," and "Bill," and the whole brave party
  Lent to thee some of their spirits rare;
 Essence of all art thou, my hearty,
  Swelling with pride in thy corner there.

Many a midnight tramp thou'st lightened,
  Chatting of dear-remembered hours;
 Many the gloomy spirit, frightened
  Out from my heart by thy kindly powers.

So in the years when my footsteps falter
  Be thou the strength that my days shall lack,
 Born of the ties no fate can alter,
  Of "Simp," and "Biler," and "Doc," and "Quack."
                              W. D. Quint, '87.

ASCUTNEY.

*A*MONG the hills that girt around
   The college and the college town,
Lies blue Ascutney's hazy peak,
Where dreamy thoughts and fancies seek
To fill each grotto with a shrine
Peopled from an unknown time.
Across the plain from college halls
Thy sunset beauty holds, enthralls,
And seems a calm, complete ideal —
A master's painting 'mid the real.
No rugged slopes or grandeur bold
Command the traveller to behold,
But softer, gentler strokes of time
Have made of thee a gem sublime.

W. B. PLUMER, '96.

WILLIAM BLAISDELL PLUMER, '96.

THE OLD SNOWSHOES.

THERE they hang above the mantel;
  Over them a rifle shines;
Underneath, a leather knapsack
  Brings a dream of other times.

Gone the study walls and windows,
  Gone the glowing student lamp;
Come the swaying branches sifting
  Moonlight on a hunter's camp.

Once again I hear the whisper
  Of the wind through mountain trees,
See the sparks from crackling embers
  Floating upward in the breeze.

From the valley comes the piercing
  Echo of the black-cat's cry,
Rising toward the blazing planet
  Marching down the western sky.

When the winter sunrise gilds the
  Granite crest of Bigelow
Over still Megantic marshes
  Buried in Canadian snow,

Once again the snowshoes rustle,
  And the strength of frosty air
Thrills along the hunter's muscles,
  Sets the warm blood leaping there.

Through the ice of old Umbagog,
  Catching salmon from the shoals;
By the birchy shores of Suncook,
  Broiling partridge on the coals;

Stalking moose along the Churchill,
  Where the hoot-owl hoarsely calls
Through the spruce and hemlock forests
  As the dusk of evening falls.

All these forest scenes have faded —
  Like the morning mists they go;
Study walls are dim in shadow,
  For the lamp is burning low.

There the snowshoes high are hanging,
  Dry and dusty on the wall,
And the hour of midnight's sounding
  Loudly over roof and wall.

                    P. E. STANLEY, '93.

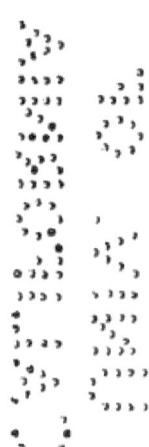

ISAAC JOSLIN COX, '96.

His Decision.

"SAY, John, are you going to set 'em up?" said George Hanson, laughing, as he pointed toward a building a short distance away.

John Harlow smiled as he glanced at the unique log structure. "Old Times Distillery Co., Louisville, Ky.," he repeated, reading the sign on the front. "No, it's against my principles to set the boys up to whiskey, but we'll take a look inside, if you want to."

"All right, come ahead," was the careless reply, as Hanson started in the direction of the building.

"Sold again!" he ejaculated gloomily, as he entered it, and saw from the quantity of débris scattered around, that the still was not yet in operation. "This is a great Fair, isn't it?" he continued. "Here it's been going two weeks, and not half of the exhibits are in position. Even a distillery can't 'set itself up' in good shape."

"Well, that pun of yours doesn't help matters at all," rejoined Harlow. "Here comes the 'Colonel' himself. Let's hear what he's got to say about his business," he added, as a portly man, whose countenance clearly proclaimed his connection with the establishment, advanced from the rear of the room.

"Good morning, gentlemen," was his courteous greeting. "I am very sorry that my still is not in operation yet, but, if you wish, I will explain the process as far as possible."

"Your old-fashioned establishment is very interesting," said Harlow, by way of compliment, when they had returned to their starting-place.

"Only the building is old-fashioned," corrected the guide. "The apparatus used is of the latest standard make. Will you kindly enter your names on our register?" he added, handing the pen to Hanson.

"What are all these figures written after the addresses?" asked the latter, pointing to a page of the register.

"Oh, you want to write your guess of the number of paid admissions to the Fair during the entire season, in that column," explained the guide, handing him a card. "You see from our card that we offer fifteen barrels of whiskey to the one guessing nearest to the correct number."

"Well, here goes my guess," said Hanson, as he recorded it. "Your turn now, John. Oh, there isn't any harm in it," seeing that he hesitated.

Harlow took the pen and wrote rapidly as his friend directed.

"I think it will be all right," he said confidently to his friend as they departed. "My guess was too large, anyhow."

*   *   *   *   *   *   *   *

John Harlow sat in his room moodily watching the falling snow, which obscured his view of the nearest college buildings.

"I should like to know how I'm to get money enough to come out square this term. Father's sick and can't help me, and I can't borrow any. Guess I'll have to leave college."

Just then he caught sight of a person beating his way along against the driving wind.

"There comes George Hanson," he exclaimed. "I hope he's got a letter for me."

A moment later Hanson came to the door and tossed a letter to Harlow, at the same time calling out, "Hallo, John! there's a letter for you."

"Thanks, old man, won't you come in?"

"No, I can't stop. I've got to plug that confounded Greek," was Hanson's mournful reply as he closed the door.

"Louisville, Ky.," said Harlow, as he glanced at the postmark, "I wonder what this is about."

His wonder did not decrease as he opened the letter and read its contents.

"By Jove!" he burst out at last. "This is a great note! My guess was the nearest right after all, and I get the fifteen barrels of whiskey. I don't know whether to call that a God-send or not."

A puzzled expression came on his face as he read the letter a second time.

"Fifteen barrels of whiskey!" he repeated to himself. "That must be worth more than a thousand dollars. I won't have to leave college after all."

He became thoughtful again, when he considered how the acceptance of such a prize might affect his standing among his college chums.

"Hang it all," he cried excitedly, rising from his chair and pacing rapidly back and forth. "They needn't know anything about it. The company write that they will dispose of it, and send me the proceeds. I don't have to tell any one where the money came from."

6

Yet he paused in his walk, as he reflected on what his parents would say about the matter. Although they would probably leave the ultimate decision with him, he was too fond of them to do anything which they might disapprove.

"Well, I don't see what I shall do. If I don't accept the prize, I'll have to leave college, and if I do the folks at home won't like it, and my influence in college will be hurt. When I get the money, I can help my folks and pay all my college bills, too. Isn't that enough good to counteract all the evil arising from it?"

But it seemed impossible for him to silence his scruples by any such pretext, although it was equally hard for him to contemplate the giving up of all hopes of an education for which he had labored so earnestly. He knew that he must decide upon one of these two courses, but as the inward struggle continued he grew more and more perplexed. "What shall I do?" he groaned aloud.

A determined look came over his face. "I won't do it," he uttered aloud.

He seated himself at his desk and rapidly penned a reply to the company, informing them concerning his decision. Later that afternoon, when John Harlow mailed two letters at the post office, one would not have imagined that anything unusual had occured.

I. J. Cox, '96.

THE OCEAN.

BENEATH the glories of a summer sky
  The mighty ocean lies in calm repose,
Its waves are still, **and** out upon **the deep**
The white-winged **ships upon their missions fly.**

A change comes **o'er the surface** of the **deep:**
Dark clouds portend the coming of the **storm;**
The sea-gulls' cries reëcho far and wide,
And mariners **a** watchful vigil keep.

And now it breaks! **In** awful rage and grand
The ocean hurls defiance at the sky,
While vivid lightning's flash and thunder's roar
Reveal the mighty power **of** God's hand.

The storm has ceased. Out **from their havens glide**
The ships, once more to fly upon their way,
While o'er the **waves,** in other voice, the calm
Proclaims again His power o'er wind and tide.

                                    W. **A. FOSTER, '95.**

THE FIRST HISTORIAN OF AMERICAN
LITERATURE.

DARTMOUTH is fond of counting its **priorities**; nor is the **task** difficult. A pleasant primacy, though **perhaps not a** commanding one, is brought **to** mind **by the recent hanging,** among **the** portraits of **the** alumni **in Wilson Hall, of a painting of** Samuel Lorenzo **Knapp, by the old-time and justly noted artist, John Vanderlyn.**

   The portrait is, from the artistic **standpoint, one of the best in the** collection **of** which it **now becomes a part;** ˌbut its chief interest **is** a personal **one. Knapp was not only a** voluminous writer, in general, **but he was the first** to produce **a book bearing the words** "American Literature" on its title-page, **and definitely** professing to give a historical account of that literature. **Of** such works—omitting cyclopædias, **collections, selections,** biographies, etc.,—there are now on my **shelves no less than nineteen, in English, German, and Italian, of which the latest bears date of 1894; but the pioneer in the list is the plainly printed and soberly bound** " Lectures **on American Literature, with Remarks on some passages of American** History. **By Samuel L. Knapp.** Published **by Elam Bliss, No. 107 Broadway. 1829.''**

CHARLES FRANCIS RICHARDSON, '71.

It is a small octavo of exactly 300 pages, and consists of a preface, fifteen lectures, a postscript, and an appendix.

Samuel Lorenzo Knapp, its ambitious writer, was born in Newburyport, graduated at Dartmouth in 1804, studied law, edited periodicals, and "wielded a facile pen" in the production of many books, too hastily prepared, or too ephemeral in theme to deserve or attain any long life. Of these the public has impartially forgotten his fiction and his biographies, save that it occasionally buys a copy of his story of the career of his eccentric fellow-townsman, Lord Timothy Dexter, of warming-pan fame. To write hasty sketches of persons or periods was a favorite pastime of Knapp's, and these accounts, though discursive rather than profound, were neither unintelligent nor unoriginal. Like so many Americans of his day, he was inclined to be over-enthusiastic in his portrayals; but those were times when America's budding glories were not nipped by many chilling frosts of local criticism, and Knapp merely followed the current custom. He wished to develop what Longfellow, in the title of his Commencement oration, just four years previous, had called "Native Writers"; and this wish was shared by his publisher, Elam Bliss, whose name appears on the title-page of other good books of the time.

That the year 1829 was a bad date in which to discuss our literature cannot be denied; it was "betwixt and between"—too early for discussion of our later and greater authors, yet just after some of them had made their beginnings. Knapp, therefore, did not discuss Longfellow, Emerson, Poe, Holmes, Hawthorne, or the histo-

rians: though he said something too much concerning
the colonial worthies and unworthies, and briefly considered such young men, or recent celebrities, as Bryant,
Cooper, and Irving. Having ample space, accordingly,
he began these lectures on American literature with the
condition of ancient Britain, and ended them with a long
account of the history of American arms on land and
sea. But, in the first discussion, if his linguistic and
sociological knowledge was sadly defective, he at least
connected literature with race, and race with environ-
ment; while, in his three closing lectures, he found one
American spirit in arms, on the rostrum, and in the
study.

The style was quasi-Johnsonian in its antitheses, and
certainly Yankee in its florid laudations or prophecies.
Furthermore, as I have said, Knapp wrote with facility
de omnibus rebus et quibusdam aliis, and never seemed
to know what to omit: American literature, in his appa-
rent view, began everywhere and would never end any-
where. But there was method in his multiplicity; he
connected literature with life, and clearly saw, and intel-
ligently said, that the flowering of a nation is the result
of long causes in a diversified garden. In some char-
acterizations—as those of Bradford's History of Plymouth Plantation (which, of course, he knew only by
extracts), Edwards on the Will, and the methods and
attainments of the revolutionary orators—he displayed
a firm hand, a critical faculty, a sense of proportion, and
an impartiality based on original reading. Dr. Knapp
(he was an LL. D. of Paris) at least showed that Dartmouth men were interested in books, and that they

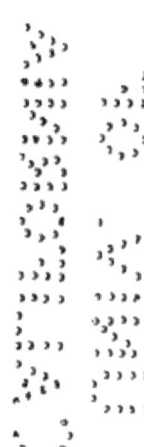

WILBUR DANIEL SPENCER, '95.

firmly believed, even in that nascent period, in the existence and endurance of such a thing as an American literature.

C. F. Richardson, '71.

Tomorrow.

THERE is a day which never comes
    To light the morning sky,
But in our thoughts alone it lives
    And there may never die;
It holds our hopes of future bliss,
    Our aspirations high,
And life itself is but a point
    In that eternity —
        Tomorrow.

Each sunset brings us nearer that
    Which earth shall not behold,
Where, far away beyond the hills
    And through the clouds of gold,
We see a glimpse of brighter hours
    Than tongue of bard has told,
When marks of time will be effaced,
    When men will not grow old —
        Tomorrow.

W. D. Spencer, '95.

Arnaut de Marueil.

THE fame of Dante illumines the ages, but his masters
in poetic art, like too many teachers of other arts
than verse, are little remembered. This is not his
fault, however. He has taken pains to acknowledge his
indebtedness to Provencal poets, and pays them the
signal compliment of introducing in his Divine Comedy
a stanza written in their tongue. Petrarch, also, is out-
spoken in his praise of them. Among those whom he
calls by name is Arnaut de Marueil.

This poet, born not far from Perigueux, in the days of
Robin Hood, loved Adalasia, vicomtesse of Beziers; and
his poetry is a record of the birth and growth of his
passion, and of its unhappy end. He was discarded for
a rival, but had the dismal comfort of being sacrificed for
a King, Alfonse of Aragon.

The verses that follow illustrate his manner and his
art. It will be observed that only four rhymes are used
in the thirty-two lines.

> Sweet to me is April, bearing
>   Winds that o 'er me softly blow;
> Rossignols their songs preparing
>   All night long in hedges low;
>   All the birds, as they have power,
>   While the dews of morning wait,
>   Sing of joy in sky and bower,
>   Each consorting with his mate.

And as all the world is airing
  New delight while new leaves grow,
It were vain to try foreswearing
  Love that sets my heart aglow :
    Both by habit and by dower
      Gladness is my rightful state;
    When dull clouds no more can lower,
      Quick my heart throws off its weight.

Helen were not worth comparing,
  Gardens no such beauty show;
Teeth of pearl, the truth declaring,
  Blooming cheeks, a neck of snow,
    Tresses like a golden shower,
      Courtly grace, for treason hate,—
    God, who bade her thus o 'ertower
      All the rest, her way make straight!

Kindness may she do me, sparing
  Courtship long and favor slow,
Give a kiss to cheer my daring—
  More, if more I earn, bestow;
    Then the path where pleasures flower
      We shall tread nor slow nor late,
    For such hopes my heart o 'erpower
      When her charms I contemplate.
                    JUSTIN H. SMITH, '77.

THE UNDECIDED BET.

ONE day, while speaking to a party of friends, I remarked that I did not see any excitement in horse racing.

"Do you ever bet on the races?" asked some one quickly, and I replied that I never did.

"Well," he continued triumphantly, "no wonder, that is the interesting part of it."

Although unaware of it at the time, I afterwards discovered that he had struck the key-note of the success of horse racing.

While this may be a little out of the line of this story, it illustrates a point I wish to emphasize in the beginning, i. e., the interest which centres around a bet.

Dartmouth has always been renowned through her athletics, and her teams have always made a good showing against the largest of the Eastern Colleges. On the track team we had, in George Radbourn, the finest half-miler that had ever entered college. When he entered, he was entirely unfamiliar with the cinder track, but, by that steady perseverance which conquers all things, he achieved a place in the front rank among prominent athletes.

Junior year George returned to college, determined to break all previous records. When he began training, he

BURPEE CALDWELL TAYLOR, '97.

found he had a dangerous rival in Tom Creighton, a Sophomore, who had entered from another college. For some unknown reason Creighton became intensely jealous of George, and the two rivals created no small amount of attention among the great body of students who were interested in athletics.

The difference between the two athletes was very marked. George was a heavily built fellow of medium height, with large strong legs, and with a fine chest development. His legs, which were almost as large above the ankles as around the calves, gave him a powerful stride. And he owed most of his success to strict, conscientious training, coupled with an unusual amount of " sand."

Tom, on the other hand. was entirely different. He was a tall, handsome fellow, with plenty of money, and a man conscious of his own abilities. He had long, wiry legs, and an enormous lung capacity, which, however, had become lessened by excessive cigarette smoking. On the track, he ran with a long, springy stride, and, in short, he was what is called an ideal runner.

Such, in short, were the two runners. George, for the most part, worked for the honor of old Dartmouth, while Tom seemed to run merely for the gratification of his own vanity.

As the day of the Fall meet approached, the rivalry between the friends of the two athletes waxed hot. A few days before the race came off, a party of students in front of the Wheelock were discussing the respective merits of the two men, when Creighton appeared upon the scene. Stepping up to one of George's most ardent

supporters he remarked, "Look here, if you think Radbourn can beat me, all right; but I have fifty dollars
that says he can't. If you have any sporting blood in
you, you will cover it; if you haven't, put up or shut
up."

A murmur of approval went through the crowd of
Creighton's supporters as he made the offer. ·The fellow
spoken to turned pale for a moment, and then, slowly
drawing out a pocket-book, remarked: "I am always
capable of backing up my own statements, and if you
want to add another fifty to that, now is your chance."

It was Creighton's turn to be surprised. For once he
had run up against the wrong man. The enthusiastic
supporter of George was none other than Clyde Mery-
field, the millionaire sport from Washington. The
money was placed and the affair finally reached George's
ears.

October 10th, the day of the meet, found the two rivals
in the best of condition. George felt in his own mind
that he could beat Tom, but still, for private reasons, he
did not wish to do so. He thought the matter over
seriously for awhile and then decided upon a certain
course.

The track was in elegant condition. It had been rolled
as smooth and hard as human hands could make it.
The starters for the half mile were soon brought out.
Such a feeling as inspires a man before a race of this
sort, only one who has participated can know. Tom's
blanched cheeks showed the nervousness which he tried
to conceal. George was apparently cool and firmly resolved upon his purpose.

Finally, the other participants had their handicaps assigned, while Tom and George were placed at the scratch. The starter's voice rang out clear and loud, "Are you ready?" No answer, "On your marks, set," Bang! went the pistol and they were off. It was plainly evident that the interest of the spectators was centred on the two rivals. Slowly but surely they were over-hauling the handicap men. At the end of the first quarter they had passed the bunch, aud then the real race began, with Creighton leading. George knew he had a hard race before him and held his strength, close behind his rival. With regular, even strides, they passed the two-twenty mark, and only two-twenty more to run. On both sides the cheering was loud, aud still like clock-work those two forms kept on. They had passed the curve and were making the final effort. Like hundred-yard men they flew down the stretch, breast with breast. The cheering for an instant ceased, and then began with renewed vigor as George, within twenty yards of the finish, put forth a supreme effort and distanced his rival by fully two yards. But, as he was about to breast the worsted, he suddenly sprang aside and let Creighton win. Tom had won his bet.

The storm of applause which was bursting forth in honor of George, was changed into a great commotion when the spectators perceived what had been done.

Tom was angry at the outcome, but the affair was done so quickly he had not the power to stop himself. The record was broken and Tom had won his bet. But · did he win it? There was a question for him to consider.

The judges declared all bets off, and praised both men

for their gamy fight.   When Tom thought the matter
over seriously, he saw the true man there was in his
rival, and, like the gentleman he proved to be, apolo-
gized to George that evening.   After the reconciliation of
the two rivals, there were not two better friends in college than George Radbourn and Tom Creighton.

B. C. Taylor, '97.

May Musings.

BRIGHT the sunlight sheds afar
 A wealth of brilliancy.
Does it kiss the lips where the roses are,
 The lips of my love, for me?

Soft the balmy zephyrs blow
 Through ev'ry budding tree.
Do they breathe a message, sweet and low,
 From the lips of my love to me?

Buoyant seems the new-born spring
 With ceaseless harmony.
Does it bring more close, by its heightening,
 The heart of my love, to me?

H. B. Metcalf, '93.

THE MAIN GROUP OF THE DARTMOUTH BUILDINGS IN 1895.

THE DARTMOUTH BUILDINGS AT PRESENT.

A VIEW of the **main group of** the College buildings, as it appears **at** present, is much less peculiarly characteristic **of** Dartmouth than the **pictures** of the same group at earlier dates. Then **they** formed almost, or quite, the whole institution; a distinction which now **they** certainly cannot claim.

The most notable change in the row, since 1850, has **been the** addition of Rollins Chapel, **on** the extreme **left, and** Wilson Hall, the Library, on the right, which were built in 1885. One alteration in Dartmouth Hall is worthy of mention; that is, the arrangement of the central entrance. In former years the **organ** (the one now in Bartlett Hall) occupied a position **beside** the one door, and the platform was opposite. The seniors sat in the front benches, right **across** the room, and behind them came the other classes in order, the freshmen in the rear. This system proved the cause of endless trouble, for it afforded **an** excellent opportunity for the sophomores to kick **the departing** freshmen **down the** steps; **an** opportunity which they, of course, did not neglect. Accordingly, about 1870, the central door was fastened up and two others substituted, one on each side, and the organ and platform changed places. The classes were located as at present, the seniors in the front middle seats, the juniors on the front sides, the sophomores on the north side, and the freshmen on the south.

The removal of all the fences has improved the appearance of the yard. The old fence of the preceding picture was succeeded by a hawthorn hedge, and that, in turn, about the time of the building of the Library and Chapel, by a wire fence. The laying of the tar-concrete walks, about eight or ten years ago. was a change greatly appreciated by the students.

Prominent among the events of the last few decades in the history of the college, is the establishment of two of the associated departments, the New Hampshire College of Agriculture and the Mechanic Arts, organized in 1868 in accordance with the act of the New Hampshire legislature,—removed to Durham in 1892; and the Thayer School of Civil Engineering, founded in 1871 by Gen. Sylvanus Thayer of South Braintree, Mass., of the class of 1807.

R. H. FLETCHER, '96.

THE OLD PINE.

(May, 1895.)

IT is night upon the hill,
  And the wind all softly creeps—
Creeps softly, low and still,
  Where the old pine vigil keeps.

And the murmuring trees around
  Breathe a prayer to the midnight air,
With a faint and fitful sound,
  For the old pine dying there.

There's a rustle in the grass;
  And in silent, mournful throng,
The shades of each old class,
  Sing a last, low, farewell song.

Farewell, farewell, ye ancient pine;
  A sacred memory is thine.
Farewell to thee,
  Old college tree ;
Farewell, Old Pine.

                    W. B. PLUMER, '96.

THE OLD PINE.

LOOKED upon for years as a landmark of fabulous
age, an inherent part of the college, respected aud
revered by all who knew it, the old pine stood upon the
hill, watching over the dear old college. It was the last
of its kind, and no young shoot sprang up to take its
place, and for a century and a half it kept its vigil and
calmly watched over the early growth and later progress
of the historic institution.

Various attempts have been made by those interested
in the subject, to prove that the old pine was growing
even before the settlement of this country by the English; as one writer put it: "It was a young shoot when
our fathers landed at Plymouth in 1620," while others
have sought to link with its history the old tradition
about the three Indians meeting around the tree and
singing their farewell song.

Ex-President Samuel Colcord Bartlett doubtless knows
more about the true history of the old tree than does
any one else. He emphatically denies the story of the
planting by the three Indians, and is firm in his belief
that the tree is not more than 150 years old. In the
first place, no three Indians can be fixed upon as forming
any educated, leave-taking trio, and, as to the song
which they were supposed to have sung, that was pub-

THE OLD PINE.

lished in an old collection of poetry, *without* the following so-called "pine stanza"—

> " When these burnished locks are grey,
> Thinned by many a toil-spent day,
> When around this youthful pine
> Moss shall creep and ivy twine,
> Long may this loved bower remain,
> Here may we three meet again."

In regard to the age of the pine, Dr. Bartlett arrived at his conclusion after careful comparison with other trees in respect to height, size, rings, and other marked features. Without doubt the old pine dates back to a period earlier than the foundation of the college in 1769, and it was probably a part of the forest which covered what is now the town proper and the surrounding hills. Some of its fellows, as they lay on the ground after the first six acres had been cleared for the college buildings, measured 270 feet in length. Growing, as it did, on a ledge, it never reached such a height, yet from its commanding position it always served as a conspicuous and imposing landmark.

The actual history of the pine begins about the year 1840, when the senior class, during commencement week, gathered about the tree and passed around a pipe, from which each member took a whiff, in supposed imitation of the Indian tradition. This custom was perpetuated, and before long an address and a poem were added to the exercises and carried out down to the present day.

In 1892 the lightning struck the old tree and the top was shattered. After that it steadily failed, and last spring, when all Nature began to clothe herself anew, the old pine from its high position stood forth with reddened needles, looking as if its life had indeed burned out.

Here, for nearly sixty years, each class met to say good-bye to the dear old college; here they smoked the farewell pipe of peace and friendship; here the old tree, with the wind sighing through its branches, whispered, with siren-like voice, a plaintive adieu, mingled with alluring words of encouragement. Known by every graduate and friend of old Dartmouth, when, during the summer of 1895, the news that it had been cut down was spread abroad over the country, it seemed as if the college had lost a true and almost human friend. Coming classes can never appreciate, or feel that thrill which makes the heart-beat quicken; they can never realize the strong sentiment which existed regarding the old pine, but as this dear old friend, almost the last of the old Dartmouth, passes from the stage of action, every one is reminded of the fact that Time changes all things, and that the dear old tree, after guiding the old college to within sight of a new era and the promised land, quietly retired to make room for the New Dartmouth.

L. S. Cox, '96.

LOUIS SHERBURNE COX, '96.

TO OUR ALMA MATER.

THERE is a College deep among the hills,
  Though old in years, in spirit young and strong;
At thought of which each heart with rapture thrills,
  To Dartmouth let us raise a hearty song.
        The Dartmouth spirit
          To our song we'll bring—
        Let the world hear it,
          As challenge we fling.

Here's to Dartmouth old and hoary!
  Here's to Dartmouth ever young!
Let us sing her fame and glory,—
  Sing a song with heart and tongue,
Till the skies reëcho o'er us
With the mighty-sounding chorus,
        Throbbing proudly,
        Swelling loudly,
  Of a song as yet unsung.
Here's to Dartmouth old and hoary!
  Here's to Dartmouth ever young!

K. KNOWLTON, '94.

At Twilight.

I LOVE to dream and rest at twilight best,
  When sinks the sun beyond the crimson west,

When softly tells the swell of low, sweet bells,
The homing of the herds from dewy dells;

Then troop the ghostly shadows o'er the plain;
The wood-thrush ripples clear his silvery strain.

But best of all I love the mellow light
That ushers in the frosty autumn night,

When stirs the breeze among the rustling trees,
And sighs for sadness in the dying leaves.

I love to ramble down the village street
And see the cheery fireside's glowing heat,

The ruddy children laughing by the flames,
Some cracking nuts, or others playing games.

As one by one the cold, bright stars appear,
I turn my steps to seek the fireside's cheer.

The supper table robed in snowy white
Has merry faces round its wealth tonight.

And what care I though dead be leaf and flower,
After a walk at autumn's twilight hour?

Le B. M. Huntington, '98.

NATHANIEL LADD FOSTER, '96.

A TURKEY FEATHER.

JAMES REED was stretched luxuriously out in the chair of one of Hanover's barbers, while that worthy, who was new to his business, and, therefore, inordinately careful, lathered his face for the fourth time. The youth, who was a sophomore, appeared to be well satisfied with himself, judging from the complacent, reminiscent look upon his face. In fact, he was occupied with what were to him very pleasant thoughts, and he did not really see the chromo to which his vacant eye was directed. He was going over, in his mind, all the incidents of his successful turkey expedition of the night before. He was wondering what would be the feelings of the farmer when he went to count his fowls that morning. I am sorry to say that "Jim," as he was called by his friends, was able to see but one side of the affair, i. e., his own. For he had accepted, without question, the code of college ethics which declares that there is a distinct difference, in fact, no analogy, between the appropriation of turkeys and stealing.

While the barber was sharpening his razor, Jim glanced carelessly around the room. There were only two other occupants, one a student and the other a rather seedy representative of the agricultural class. He saw, without noticing it particularly, that the man seemed interested in the cut of his trousers, judging from the intent gaze bestowed upon them. Jim glanced complacently at the carefully creased production of the modern tailor, and then, by way of comparison, at the patched and faded ones of the farmer, and slightly smiled. As he turned his head to receive the attentions of the razor, he could see from the corner of his eye that the tiller of the soil still kept an intent and rather peculiar look upon his trousers. Looking more carefully, he discovered, somewhat to his dismay, that near the bottom, on the side next to the farmer, was a small but undoubted turkey feather. It came over his rather guilty conscience that the man must certainly be the owner of his last night's spoils. But no! How foolish he was. There was very little chance that such a coincidence should happen. And, besides, what if it was so? A mere feather didn't prove anything. But, in spite of this reasoning he could not banish a feeling of uneasiness, which was increased by the fact that the corner of his eye told him that the steady gaze of his tormentor did not abate, but, as it seemed to him, became more and more intent. He turned his face so that the barber could shave the opposite side, and this put the man out of the line of his vision. But the relief was only momentary, as he could seem to feel that the feather was still the cynosure of those eyes. He thought of brushing it off with his other leg, but saw that this would "give him away" more than ever.

The farmer now gave two or theee coughs, that sounded terribly significant to the now thoroughly alarmed student. He recalled that a senior had said, the night before, that most of the turkey owners any-

where around Hanover had vowed to send to prison any
student-thief they could catch. He pictured to himself
the distress of his parents, and, worse than all, that of a
"girl he knew." That settled it. He would try the only
way that he could see, and throw himself upon the
mercy of the man, and, by the promise of a large sum
of money, try to buy him off. Rising hastily from his
chair, for the gentleman of the razor had finally completed his task, Jim beckoned the farmer to come outside. The latter, with wonder expressed all over his
face, followed him out. At first he did not seem to
understand what the jumbled-up confession of the boy
was all about. But he did have intelligence enough to
pocket the twenty-dollar bill held out to him. Jim
finally noticed that something was wrong, and began
to think he had perhaps made a mistake after all, and
abruptly stopped and waited for the other to speak.
And this is what he heard: "Young feller, I did some
wonder where that turkey feather came from, but I
don't jest know what you mean by yer talk about
takin' my turkeys, 'cause I ain't never kep' any. But,
as fer the money, I ain't too proud to take it, and God
bless ye fer it. It 'll help me and Mary out wonderfull";
and with that he started gaily toward his broken-down
horse and wagon.

And that is why James Reed could never afterwards
be drawn into turkey parties, and why his monthly
account, which he sent home to his father, contained the
following item:

Charity..$20.00

N. L. FOSTER, '96.

MEMORIES OF HORACE.

" BEHOLD Soracte white with winter snow,"
   Ah, grand old poet of the Sabine farm,
    I never read thy memory-haunting psalm,
But what Ascutney, lying blue and low
Upon the south, and veiled in misty glow,
    Doth come to me, and all the mellow charm
    Of those long summer days of holy calm
We passed with Alma Mater long ago.

What though Soracte now with snow is white,
    What though the summer days come not again!
    Heap high the fire from Memory's plenteous store,
With summer fagots cheer the winter night,
    Fling far away the thoughts of grief and pain,
    And let our souls be jovial once more.

F. L. PATTEE, '88.

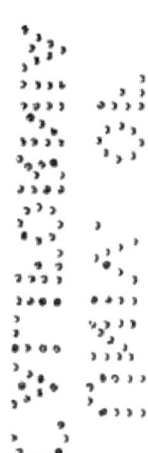

CHARLES NICHOLAS McCALL, '98.

PLEDGING A FRESHMAN.

A YOUNG Freshman once arrived at **Dartmouth College**, fresh **from** the comforts of home and the companionship of doting relatives. He felt very **lonely** as, **standing** in the hall **of** the Wheelock, where **he had** temporarily taken up his abode, he looked about at **the** strange faces **and** listened to **the** bustle and **confusion** attending **the arrival** of students. He was **almost** inclined to **think of** giving up **college and of** returning **once** more to his home. **However,** he **considered** that, **after** awhile, he would become acquainted with his fellow-students, **and** that then college life **would become** bearable, if not enjoyable.

Suddenly he **saw one of the strangers who were standing about in the** hall, **advance** toward **him, smiling** pleasantly.

"**Is** this Mr. Greene?" asked the stranger, cordially extending his hand.

The Freshman acknowledged his identity.

"I heard that you were coming," said the stranger; "**we** have been looking out for **you.** Come over here and I will introduce **you to my friend, Mr. Upsilon Psi.**"

The Freshman timidly followed his new friend to the other side of the hall, where he was introduced to a man as complete a stranger to him as had been the first. The two chatted to him very pleasantly, **on various**

matters, for a considerable time. Finally, Mr. Upsilon Psi observed, kindly laying his hand on the Freshman's shoulder:.

"Mr. Greene, we would like to take you over to our fraternity 'chin.' There are a good many of the fellows from your town in our society, and we would like you to come over, so we can see how we like you and you can see how you like us."

Mr. Greene gladly agreed to go, and thought how kind it was of these lordly Sophomores, or Juniors, or perhaps Seniors, to take so much interest in a poor lone Freshman like himself. But when he arrived at the "chin" his wonder and pleasure increased. Everyone seemed interested to hear about where he came from and to learn what his tastes were, and they gave him ice cream and cake and treated him royally. By and by he said that he must return to the Wheelock, and Mr. Upsilon Psi and the mysterious man who had first accosted him, — and whose name he did not yet know, — volunteered to escort him thither.

"How do you like our fellows?" inquired Mr. Upsilon Psi, as the three walked back together.

"Very much, indeed," replied the Freshman; "you've treated me finely, and I am ever so much obliged to you."

"Oh, don't mention it," said the mysterious man, "but now, see. You say you like our fellows; I can assure you that they like you. Now, why should you wait any longer? Why not pledge tonight to join our society?"

"Well," said Mr. Greene, somewhat embarrassed, "I

promised to go down **to a** Φ Δ A 'chin' tomorrow **night, so** I'm afraid I'll have to wait till after that."

"Oh, very well," said the mysterious man, somewhat reproachfully, "of course, if you like. But when you're 'chinned' by a society like Υ Ψ, it is not a time to hesitate or delay."

"No, of course not," replied the Freshman, hurriedly; "but, you see, I've promised and I can't very well help going."

"No, I suppose not," said Mr. Upsilon Psi, magnanimously; "well, we'll see you after tomorrow night. Here we are at the door. Good-night."

"Good-night," said Greene; "thank you very much for your kindness."

But the Freshman was not yet to retire to his lonely room. In the hotel hall he met a man who introduced himself as Mr. Epsilon Deeke, who was very cordial and friendly, and who insisted on hauling him off to another "chin" that same evening, despite the Freshman's plea of having some algebra to study. At the "chin" Mr. Deeke and his friends sang the praises of the E K Δ fraternity; and, on hearing of the Freshman's previous experience, warned him, with every appearance of anxious interest in his welfare, that, though Υ Ψ was, undoubtedly, a fine society, and many of its members fine fellows, still it was a well-known fact that it contained some of the most notorious "sports" in college. He also had it duly impressed upon him that E K Δ was the largest society in the country and had the greatest number of chapters, and that, in Dartmouth, it had the best representation on the athletic teams, and on the dramatic and the musical clubs. It was full twelve o'clock that night when Mr. Greene threw his tired form upon his bed in the Wheelock.

The next evening, in spite of the counter attraction of a foot-ball rush, he proceeded, under the kind care of Mr. Alfadelt, to the "chin" of the fraternity of Φ Δ A. Here the scenes of the preceding evening were repeated, and everyone was attentive, interested, and kind. They asked him by what societies he had already been "chinned," and, when he told them, gave him some useful information about these fraternities. E K Δ, he was told, was a nefarious organization, and, in its anxiety to increase its numbers, used methods to induce Freshmen to pledge, which at once gained it the contempt of the glorious Φ Δ A society. "As for Υ Ψ," said Mr. Kressent, one of the leading Φ Δ A men, "well, we call it our equal, and we two are certainly the best societies in college; but," he added confidentially, and speaking in a lower tone, "Υ Ψ has been going down hill lately, as some of the men admitted last year show. Now, ours is the oldest living Greek Letter Society; its distinguished members are scattered all over the country, and the man who joins it will never have reason to regret it."

"And then look at our pin," said Mr. Alfadelt, proudly pointing to his own, "isn't it a beauty?" Why, all the other societies envy us and confess we have a prettier pin than any of them."

Mr. Greene was duly impressed by this important argument in favor of joining the society.

A vigorous attack was then made upon the Freshman. Mr. Kressent, ably assisted by Mr. Alfadelt, Mr.

N. Thusiast, and Mr. Starr, talked to him for about half
an hour, and so fired **him** with enthusiasm by the many
tales of the glory of the fraternity, the brotherly love
existing within **it, and** the magnificent literary advan-
tages offered, that, unwilling to let such a wonderful opportunity slip, and fearful that delay might injure his
chances of admission, he pledged. Soon after he returned to the Wheelock, happy and pleased with himself,
and, as he took off his coat, preparatory **to** retiring,
glanced with pride at the pledge button which **one** of his
kind Φ Δ A friends had placed **in** his button-hole.

The **next week was one of hard work to the Fresh-**
man, and he did not see many **of those who had been so**
kind to him. He noticed, indeed, that **he** was **not so**
much sought after as before, and **he** had few callers, save
that one or another **of** his Φ Δ A friends would drop in
occasionally, still kind and pleasant, though perhaps not
quite so beaming as on the night of the "chin."

One day **he met Mr.** Upsilon Psi and the mysterious
man (whose name **was** Dyamund, he had discovered,)
walking **down the street.** He bowed pleasantly, but
there was little response. Mr. Upsilon Psi **gave** him
a cold, pitying smile, and the mysterious man gazed
dreamily down the street. Mr. Deeke, too, whom he
met often, seemed strangely indifferent about his welfare.

"Well," said the Freshman, philosophically, "my Φ Δ A
friends will stick by me."

But in two months this fact had ceased **to** give much
comfort. They had stuck by him, indeed. He had given
to Mr. Kressent a good-sized check for a pin, **and to** Mr.
Starr some cash down for an initiation fee. **With money**

gone, and more, perhaps, to go, and with the terrors of initiation **looming** up before him, the Freshman **began** to **wonder if secret** societies were such fine things, **after** all, or if they did not partake somewhat of the character of frauds.

Did he find anything to repay him when he got **inside?** It is doubtful. He has not told.

C. N. McCall, '98.

A Glance.

A PAIR of eyes I saw but **once**
　　Are looking into mine,
And in their play,
The laughter gay
And tender grace together shine,
　　As when I saw them beaming there.

Come, Cupid, tell your **captive where**
　Their owner dwells today,
　That I may thither stray,
　And drink again the dazzling **wine**
That sparkles **with a wealth divine,**
　Within two eyes I saw but once.

H. B. Metcalf, '93.

HARRY BINGHAM METCALF, '93.

THE OLD CLOCK.

WITH all thy memories and all
    Thy moments dear to me,
Old Clock upon the college **hall,**
    My heart goes out to thee;
Four fleeting years, no longer thine,
    Since time ran on apace,
Four golden years, I count as mine,
    While thou and I were face to face.

But Time, which conquers all **at length,**
    Has conquered thee, old friend,
And all thy pride and early **strength**
    Are coming to an end;
Thy weary hands are sometimes slow,
    Or cease to move at all,
While shadows come and shadows go
    Along the ancient gable wall.

While others in their thoughtless **mood**
    Reproach thee for delay,
I ask thee not to make it good
    If thou must lose a day;
Forget the later, cruel jest,
    Which careless lips have said,
Remember that they knew **thee least**—
    Thy oldest friends have long been **dead.**

Men have their many holidays
  And periods of rest,
And still they weary of their ways
  And lose their youthful zest;
So thou, Old Clock, for faithful zeal
  Thy tired hands may stay,
And rest thee for thy better weal
  In an eternal holiday.

W. D. SPENCER, '95.

A NOCTURNE.

THE soft and sylph-like shadows throw
  A robe about the dying day,
And dark-eyed night, with laughter low,
  Trails in the sky her glittering train.

The soft, sweet-scented western wind
  Seems but the breath of lovely night,
As through the latticed, open blind,
  It woos me with its whisperings.

The soothing voice of rippling streams,
  The music of the meadow marsh,
But lulls me with delicious dreams,
  And I am lost in slumberland.

LE B. M. HUNTINGTON, '97.

LeBaron Monroe Huntington. '98.

A QUESTION OF ETHICS.

IT is often repeated that college students live in a world of their own, a world whose events and problems, sometimes at least, differ **very** materially from those of all other places. Perhaps **the contrast is more** in appearance **than in reality, in form than in** fundamental principle. However this may be, **there** are certain kinds of experiences for whose exact likeness we must certainly seek in vain amid any but academic surroundings. Of such is an incident recently related to me by **a middle-aged gentleman** with whom **I** chanced to strike **up a** travelling acquaintance. **He had been relating several** of his exploits, performed during an active career **at one** of **our New** England institutions, and my **interest was** already **at** a high pitch, when, after a few **moments of** meditation, he commenced upon this:

"The strangest and most serious predicament that I was ever involved in while in college," he said, "was the very last. This was the **way** of it: The trouble all began with a circumstance no less trival than the failure of our librarian to note the return **of a book** that I had drawn. I can remember just how that **volume looked —** a red-covered edition **of** 'Marmion,' with the **name in** big fancy letters **on** the **cover.** Well, in consequence of **the** Professor's carelessness, **it remained on the list** charged to **me. This error could easily have been dis-**

covered, of course, if there hadn't been any complications; but, as it was, another fellow happened to steal the same identical volume, a few days after I had taken it back—though few such thefts were successfully committed with us—and that was the real cause of the row.

"This was at the beginning of the last term of Senior year. About two months later I received notice, much to my surprise, that 'Marmion' was long overdue. I protested that I had returned it, but to no use; the absence of the book from the library shelves corroborated the records. Even under such circumstances my word might have sufficed, if my conduct during my course had been reasonably good; but the truth is, as you have seen, that I was always a rather harum-scarum sort of a rascal, and could hardly expect to be trusted against such evidence. Still, I thought that since Commencement was so near, the affair might come to nothing; but in this I was disappointed. The faculty was particularly anxious to put a stop to the habit of pilfering before it became general, and met my continued assertions of innocence with a declaration that I shouldn't be allowed to graduate until I should return the missing volume or furnish another copy; in either case, of course, submitting to some disciplining besides.

"This made things look rather bad. It would be hard enough on any fellow to compel him to take his choice between proclaiming himself a thief and a liar when he was neither, or else forfeiting his degree; but it was especially unfortunate for me. My father, knowing my natural proclivities, had sent me to college as a sort of an experiment. He had especially told me, when I entered, that if I got my diploma he would take me with him into his business,—a large and prosperous one,—but that, if I failed to pull through, I should have to take care of myself afterwards; and I knew that he was by all odds too dogmatic and absolute to be prevented by any excuses or explanations, however plausible, from fulfilling the literal meaning of his words.

"One chance of honorable escape was still left. I happened, by mere accident, to know who it was that really had the troublesome book; so I went to him and told the story, attempting to prove, what seemed clear enough to me, that the only thing for him to do was to take back the volume and acknowledge his responsibility. I failed to convince him. As luck would have it, he was on probation, and the detection of the theft, as he said, would undoubtedly result in his expulsion. He argued that, on the other hand, I was really in no predicament at all, as I could get out of the fix completely by returning a copy of the book to the library under protest. 'For,' said he, 'if you stick it out that you didn't take it, the faculty will be convinced that you didn't anyway, so your reputation will be all right; and now they've said they won't let you graduate unless you replace the d—d thing, they won't.'

"The truth of the latter statement I realized only too well. The former I knew to be unwarranted, but I could not persuade him that such was the case. I kept talking on in despair, and at last even threatened to denounce him; but I had my trouble for my pains. He knew well enough that I wouldn't actually go so far as that. 'Denounce, then, and be a sneak,' he said,

''Twon't be any worse for me than if I confess myself,' he added. The logic of that remark was unanswerable, I knew, in the eyes of such a fellow as he; so I wasted no more breath on him.

"Only two alternatives now remained, for the false sense of honor made me dismiss at once the idea of really giving information against the culprit. I might refuse to comply with the conditions for my graduation imposed by the faculty, and throw away my chances for a quick rise in business; or I might return to the library a copy of 'Marmion,' and thus, in the eyes of the college, exchange my honor for the degree—for, in spite of any number of protests, everyone would have regarded such a course as practically an admission of guilt. The question was, whether my reputation with the few hundred individuals who made up the students and faculty was worth the sacrifice I must undergo to keep it clean. I spent a good while in deliberation, and for a long time I was undecided. Finally my pride gained the upper hand. I went to the President and told him that I had positive knowledge that the book had been stolen by another fellow; that I would never plead guilty to a false accusation, and that I would not reveal the name of the thief. The result was as I expected; the professors were inflexible, and would not allow me to receive a degree.

"It would, doubtless, have made a more dramatic story if this incident had ruined all my subsequent life; but that was not the case. Though I was thrown at once on my own resources, and though the death of my father, three years later, put an end to the idea that I might finally get into his business after all, which some small measure of success had put into my head—'Hope springs eternal in the' (what is it?) 'human breast,' you know—still, I think I have made my way nearly as well as I should have done in company with him. Nevertheless, it has always been a question with me, and I suppose it always will be, whether, considering the circumstances, I really made the most rational decision. What do you think about it?"

R. H. FLETCHER, '96.

WHAT CARE I?

WHAT care I if the cruel world
   Shows its harsher side to me?
What care I if fortune fickle
   Turns her back, nor smiles on me?
What care I if troubles come,—
   Friends desert me—old and new?
What care I for all these things
   If one loving heart be true?

H. S. BAKETEL, D. M. C.

APPLE BLOSSOMS.

UNDER the apple tree standing,
  Peeping half slyly from covert so green;
Fairest of all the waving **May** blossoms,
  Maiden, half hidden, half seen!
The full **joyous** notes of springtime welling,
Thy praises alone to my heart are telling.

Beauteous **apple tree blossoms**!
  Flowers **by May** day's breezes **soft stirred**;
Fluttering so lightly down from **the branches**,
  Shaken by wandering bird;
Thy pink and white tints in harmony blending,
  A message of joy to my heart are sending.

Fragrant and quick-fading blossoms!
  Mingling thy perfume with eve's gentle dew!
Crown with the beauty of languishing petal
  My darling, so tender, so true,
Affection's own soul! whose love enduring,
Eternity's bliss to my heart's **assuring**.

                                    I. J. Cox, '96.

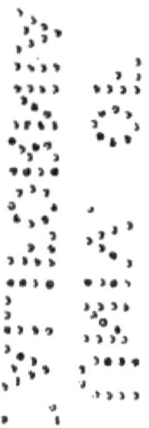

SHERMAN ROBERTS MOULTON, '98.

John Freeman.

I KNEW John Freeman very well. He was in my class, that of 186-, and we were thrown together very much, since the Dartmouth of those days was not so large as now. John was a typical New Englander, tall, raw-boned and strong, with an honest, open face that made you instinctively feel that he was a man to be trusted. He was "slow in speech and slow in wrath," and a hard worker, for he was poor and must make his way in the world.

A direct contrast to him in most points was his room-mate and chum, Harry Fitzhugh, of Richmond, Virginia. Harry was rather short, dark and wiry, and in temperament a regular Southerner. He had one of the finest tenor voices in college, and many times have I listened to his singing, accompanied with many a false note from his room-mate's banjo.

It seemed surprising to many, that two men so unlike as John and Harry should be such friends. Indeed, they said that the only point that the two held in common was the love of truth. The reason of their friendship was this. One day, while skating on the Connecticut, Harry had ventured upon some thin ice, which had broken under his weight, and he would probably have been drowned had not John come to the rescue. This had happened in the winter of their Freshman year, and from that time they were hardly ever separate, until the event came which was to change the course of their lives—the civil war.

There was great excitement in the little New England college when the news of the firing upon Fort Sumter reached Hanover, and all realized that the war had, in truth, begun. Those Southerners who had not already gone home now did so, and among the number was Harry Fitzhugh. It was hard for him to say good-bye to John, and the two vowed eternal friendship, and each promised to aid the other if in trouble. Then they parted, and John went to enlist in the regiment which was being organized at his home.

The rest of the story is known by hearsay alone. Harry Fitzhugh went steadily up in the scale of rank, until, in 1863, he was made colonel for gallantry upon the field. Indeed, so brave was he, that when a man was needed for a particularly important and perilous mission, he was naturally the man selected. Entering the Union lines in disguise, he succeeded in discharging his business, and had all but escaped, when he was discovered and pursued. Wounded by a shot from his pursuers, he stumbled and fell, but the enemy had lost track of him, and for a time he was secure. Later on, however, he was discovered, lying behind a log, by one of the soldiers, who was none other than his old college chum, John Freeman. Filled with pity for the wounded man, and the ties of friendship triumphing over the demands of duty, John helped him to escape. The two friends never met again. John fell in a skirmish only two days afterwards, and Harry, who told me this tale, is living now in Richmond.

S. R. MOULTON, '98.

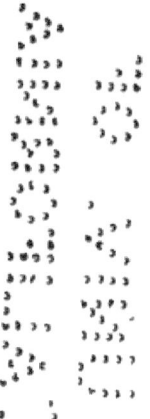

OLD DARTMOUTH HALL.

DARTMOUTH HALL SPEAKS.

TO be torn down!
   So soon forgotten all our past?
A century of struggles classed
As naught? And, Dartmouth, when at last
We 've won, you 'd tear me down.

      To be torn down!
Sons of "Old Dartmouth," you 're my own.
Will you see me thus overthrown?
Your boasted love for me outgrown
So soon? Then tear me down.

      To be torn down!
No, Honored College, vain my fears!
A parent weighed by honored years
Is safe. A century's love endears
Too well to be crushed down.

                    F. V. BENNIS, '98.

A College Picture.

IT is autumn, and college life has again begun. It is early dawn and quiet broods over the slumbering village. The golden beams of the morning sun rise peacefully from their hiding, over the beautiful eastern hills, and shed their benediction on the old group of classic structures. They seem to kiss the blushing foliage of the historic maples and scintillate in regal splendor among the crystal drops of dew. Mists are dissipating from the campus, a dense bank of fog is hovering o'er the river and all is still.

*   *   *   *   *   *   *   *

The evening songs have been sung. The occasional blow on the table, as the winning card goes down, is no longer heard. The midnight "feed" is over. The latest nocturnal rambler has returned and drawn his nightly shroud about him. All, from the jolly fat man to the gravest old "plugger," are enjoying that last sweet repose on the boundary between night and day. A calm and peaceful serenity rests on the scene. There is not a stir, nor a voice. All is still—gravely still—still like death—the only quiet hour in a college town.

*   *   *   *   *   *   *   *

In an instant all is changed. Out peal the tones of the old college bell, echoing in startling reverberations

JOHN HENRY BARTLETT, '94.

through chamber and hall. Hundreds of classic sleepers spring from their couches, suddenly aroused to thoughts of breakfast, chapel, and studies. From every dormitory they pour forth. The campus is alive with lines of hurrying forms, scarcely yet awake to life. And yet they continue to come, hastily darting from the doors, as the sleepy eyes are pulled through the sweater, until the latest slumberer is in action.

*　　*　　*　　*　　*　　*　　*　　*

Soon the lines of humanity are reversed. In a studious mood all are wending their ways toward the chapel. Again strikes up the bell. All paces quicken. The last fifteen warning strokes begin. The rear of the line is on the run. They are fast counting off the strokes. A few stragglers are sprinting down the campus. Alas, the double stroke—the doors close with an ominous bang. At the Rood House corner the sprinters stop in despair, sigh for breath, grieve for another "cut," and the comedy of the morning has been played.

J. H. BARTLETT, '94.

"WOODIN' UP."

Our daddies set the custom,
(Ah, bless 'em, how we trust 'em,)
A-stamping fit to bust 'em,
    Woodin' up!

Let roll the *soleful* thunder
At Dick's all-harmless blunder.
"Get up!" What horse? we wonder,
    Woodin' up!

The good pine floors have stood it
While class on class have wood it.
Let die the custom! Could it,
    Woodin' up?

No, no! Let 's go out dusty
From our Dartmouth, good and trusty,
And our custom never rusty,
    Woodin' up!

G. A. GREEN, '98.

AN EXPERIENCE WITH THE RHO KAP'S.

IT was raining hard, and Boston on **a wet** night is a most disagreeable city. Washington **and** Tremont streets were crowded with hurrying people. It **was one** of those cold September nights which give **warning of** the coming winter. **At every** fresh **gust of** wind **the** traveller buttoned **his coat more** tightly about him and hastened toward **home.**

One **stranger** alone seemed to **be in no hurry, as he** stood **gazing** about him, debating whether **or** not **he** should **proceed. He** did not long hesitate, **however, as** a **big,** red-nosed patrolman came along just **then, and** cried out:

"Come, get a move **on, will** yer; don't block up the sidewalk that way."

The **stranger, a large** countrified-looking chap, **who** could have **crushed** the big-waisted policeman with **one** blow, **turned, startled by** the angry command, **and** began to excuse himself. "I didn't mean any offense, sir; I was looking for the street that leads to the Union Station, and—"

"None **of yer 'back talk,' now, or I'll run yer in; see!"** broke in **the** officer.

The stranger **was** about **to** make an angry retort, but, on second thought, **turned and** went down the street.

A **bright, good-looking little** fellow, **who had heard the** conversation, hurried up to the stranger and asked if he could be of any assistance to him.

"Well," answered the big fellow, with a peculiar Western drawl, "I should like to find the Union Station, if it ain't too much trouble for you to show me."

"Why, certainly not," answered the boy; "I am going that way myself, and—here's a car now. Jump on!" After they were seated he said: "I am afraid our police are not very polite, but then you get used to that sort of thing after you have lived here awhile. Are you going to take one of the evening trains out of the city?"

"Yes, I intend to take the late train for Hanover, New Hampshire, where I am going to college."

"You don't mean to say that you are going to enter Dartmouth?"

"Yes; do you know anyone there?"

"You bet I do; my father graduated there in the sixties, and I am going up there tomorrow myself and enter as a Freshman, so I suppose we shall be classmates. How funny that we should meet in this way. Gee! but won't you make a corker for the foot-ball team?"

The stranger smiled, and said he did not know anything about the game.

"O, that don't matter much," quickly replied the other, "you 'll soon learn. But here we have been talking at a great rate and don't know each other yet.' My name is Archie Kimball; 'Shorty,' the boys over to the Latin School call me."

"And mine is Scott Raymond, from Eagle Heights, Arkansas."

"Well, here we are at the Union Station," said Archie, as they started to get out of the car, "and a good quarter of an hour before the train goes."

Everything was rush and bustle for the next few minutes, and half an hour later found the two newly-made friends on the way to their respective destinations; the one, rejoicing in his lucky acquaintance, the other, happy because he had met a future classmate.

About a week later the two friends were installed as Freshmen, and already Raymond had given promise of a great foot-ball player. The two men so oddly matched became great chums, and were to be found together almost every evening. One night, about ten o'clock, Raymond was just leaving Archie's room, when he heard a party of students coming in their direction, and caught a snatch of the song: "Rho Kap' I am, Rho Kap' I'll be, Rho Kap' through all eternity."

"That is the Sophomore hazing society," said Archie, "and they are coming over to have some fun with me, because I blew a horn after the foot-ball rush, the other night. You'd better not stay, as they may make trouble for you."

"If they touch you while I am here," returned Raymond, "there will be trouble. The cowards dare not take anyone of their own size."

"They are knocking now," said Archie. "Come in," and in walked ten or fifteen Sophs.

"We want you, Kimball," said the leader, a sportylooking fellow, with a turned-up nose and sneering mouth.

"What for?" asked Archie.

9

"No joking, Freshman; come along with us and do as you are told."

"But what if I don't propose to let him," said Raymond in his slow, drawling style, as he began to remove his coat.

"You have nothing to say about it," answered the leader angrily, and started for Archie, saying, "Come on, boys."

He had got about half-way across the room when he found his shoulder in a vise-like grasp. In less time than it takes to tell, Raymond knocked the two leaders' heads together and then grabbed those nearest him. The room was in a great state of commotion, and Rho Kap's were sprawling about in all directions. Those nearest the door sought safety in flight, and Archie looked on with wonder as his friend vented his rage on the unfortunate hazers.

"And now," said Raymond, giving the leader a final cuff, "if you or your crowd ever lay your hands on my friend, I'll trounce every one of you on sight." And he looked as if he meant every word he said.

The Rho Kap's were fully convinced that the new football star was capable of carrying out his threat, and it is needless to say that Archie Kimball was not hazed that fall.

"And to think," said Archie to his chum one day, while talking over their impressions of the first few weeks, "only think how strangely it happened that I was not 'Rho Kapped.' My little assistance to you in Boston was surely more than repaid."

B. C. TAYLOR, '97.

CHAPEL BELL.

WHAT cuts athwart the morning air,
   (Winter air !)
 Arousing me to daylight's glare,
    From my lair ?
       Chapel Bell !

What makes me chew my morning steak
   (Leathern steak !)
In haste ; some crullers grab, and make
   A speedy break ?
       Chapel Bell !

What makes me **take a morning** slide
   (Icy slide !)
Across the campus, on **the glide,**
   Feet denied ?
       Chapel Bell !
       Single strokes.
       G. A. GREEN, '98.

THE NEW QUADRANGLE.

THE greatest single change ever brought **about in** Dartmouth's external appearance will be **the erec-**tion of the proposed "quadrangle." Perhaps, however, it is hardly accurate **to speak of** this as a **single ad-**dition; for the buildings composing **the** completed whole, **as** shown **in** the picture, **will be erected at** considerable intervals **of time.**

Early **in 1894 the authorities began** to lay **plans for the** much-needed **expansion in material** equipment. As **they** decided **to work on** a **scheme** capable of sufficient increase in **the future,** they found available for **the** halls **only** three **locations. One, the portion** of Observatory **Hill between the** Medical **College and the dormitories,** would have demanded a rather crowded **arrangement in two** parallel terraces, **and would have been very expen-**sive. At present, be it remarked in passing, one build-**ing,** a physical laboratory, may soon be placed **in** that region, just to the north-east of the chapel. The second possible situation, the east side of North College street, **seemed little better than the first; the third,** and last, **was the square on which stands the church. This plan was advised by Frederick Law Olmsted & Co.,** land-**scape architects, and the proposal contemplated the purchase of the square as a whole and** the erection upon **it of a regular closed quadrangle;** but, as some of the

THE NEW QUADRANGLE.

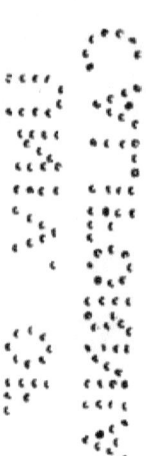

property could not be secured, the **trustees determined
to use** instead only **the** southern half and **to construct**
there a three-quarter quadrangle, including **the church,
open toward the campus.**

In the spring **of** 1895 ground **was** broken for the cen-
tral edifice, **the** Butterfield Museum of Palæontology,
Archæology, **Ethnology, and** kindred sciences, provided
for **by** the will of Dr. Ralph Butterfield, of Kansas City,
an **alumnus** of the **Class** of 1839. **This appears** in the
centre of the view. It will be finished by Commencement, 1896, **at a cost of $70,000. Its dimensions are
145 and 55 feet** respectively; **its style, Ionic; and the
materials employed** in **its construction, Lebanon granite,
"Milwaukee brick," Indiana sandstone, and terra cotta.
It will contain recitation rooms, as well as** the **collections. Next, in chronological order, will be the** Memorial Hall, which **may be begun in 1896 or 1897, and**
will occupy **a** position **corresponding on the east to
that of** the church on **the west,** about on **the** site **of the
present "Rood House."** The necessary **funds, of which
$15,000 are already** subscribed, **are** being raised **among
the alumni. Its** lower floor will **probably be occupied
by the departments** of administration, and will contain
the offices of the president, trustees, **dean, and** treasurer.
Its second story may be devoted to an auditorium, and,
in any case, will be adorned with the portraits and pictures illustrative of the history of the college. On either
side of the Museum, **the rear** of each on **a** line with the
front of the Museum, **will** stand a recitation building:
one devoted to history, political science, philosophy, and
kindred **subjects; the other to** the languages, ancient

and modern. These **three** projected structures will be
of light material, to harmonize with that of the **one**
already under construction. Before they are completed,
the houses now fronting the street will be removed and
the ground graded in a uniform slope to the level of the
campus. The interior court will be 200 feet square, an
area to be made possible by the shifting **of the** side-
walk on the east. All the buildings will be heated from
a central station. They will be connected by an inner
collonade of pillars, **and will** present **a very imposing**
appearance.

R. H. FLETCHER, '96.

"GOOD WORK!"

WHEN a man has shown himself above
    The ordinary push and shove, —
Deserves a hearty word of praise,
At Dartmouth, we've a homely phrase:
    "Good work, old man!"

The Dartmouth man, with sturdy **nerve**,
On top, and never known **to swerve**,
Awaits, in life, **the coming day**
The world shall **clap his back, and say**:
    "Good work, old man!"

G. A. GREEN, '98.

George Abbott Green, '98.

DRIFTING SONG.

WAVELETS lifting my little boat,
   Gently drifting, I lie and float
Over the boundless sea.
Wavelets plashing against my **bed**,
Thunders clashing over my head,
   Both are as one to me :
Both are as one, as I sink **to sleep**,
Roaming the deep.

Oh, the bliss **of** the surcease of pain!   .
Soothed by the kiss of the **waters, I gain**
   Peace for a moment and **rest—**
A moment's setting aside **of strife,**
A moment's forgetting of this sad life
   By sorrow oppressed,
An infinite rest for an instant to **know**
From infinite woe.

Drifting ever, I thus would stray,
Greeting never again the day,
   Through the unchanging night ;
Only waking to hear the roar
Of surges breaking upon the shore
   That fringes the realms of light ;
There, in Elysian fields, to find
Sweet peace of mind.

K. KNOWLTON, '94.

A Dartmouth Song.

DARTMOUTH, 'mid thy hills enthroned,
 Where, o'er summits purple-coned,
  The eagles soar,—
Thine the majesty we sing!
Loudly let the anthem ring,
Wide around reëchoing,—
  Dartmouth evermore.

Queen of the North! Her classic brow
Arts and sciences endow,
  And ancient lore.
Clear and bright her radiant crown,
Sheds the light of learning down,—
Spreads afar her fair renown,—
  Dartmouth evermore!

Distant lands may claim her sons,
Where the broad Missouri runs,
  Or rapids roar.
Still, however far we fly,
Love for her shall never die,—
Still we bear her banner high,—
  Dartmouth evermore!

      G. C. Selden, '93.

AN INCIDENT IN COLLEGE LIFE.

IT was a cold, frosty night of February, a few days before Washington's Birthday. A stranger to Hanover, judging from external appearances, would scarcely have supposed himself to be in a college town, for, although the evening was yet young, the streets were almost completely deserted by students.

Of course the office of the "Wheelock" contained its usual quota of "students about town," as a certain class of so-called "rag-chewers" might well be designated, who were sitting or standing in groups, discussing topics ranging from base-ball prospects to the theory of evolution or the "Evidences of Christianity."

The store-fronts, even, were subjected, for once, to a test as to their ability to stand alone, being deprived of their usual "townie" support.

But college life, in all its various in-door phases, was flowing smoothly on in the various students' rooms; and it is one of those rooms which we will now look in upon.

'Round a blazing open fire were seated three Sophomores, engaged in discussing the approaching Freshman class supper.

"I tell you," the foot-ball man was saying, "this class will be everlastingly disgraced if those blooming Fresh-

men are allowed to have their banquet, while ninety——
sits around like a flock of young lambs and does not
make a move to interfere." •

"You're dead right, me boy," put in the base-ball
man, whose language was always a trifle idiomatic.
"They have had a soft thing so far. This class is in a
trance."

"Do you remember how ninety—— tried to swipe our
toast-master last year? How he escaped through the
back window while his room-mate held forty Sophs. at
bay, and how the whole class kept guard for —"

"What, again?" This last came from an athletic
young fellow who had been stretched at ease on the
window-seat, apparently asleep.

"You fellows make me more tired than one of B——'s
lectures," he said, slowly raising himself to a sitting
posture. "This is about the fiftieth time this week I
have heard this same talk. Now, I have a little proposal to make, which will decide whether or not you are
so anxious to do something for the honor of ninety——.
It is this: I will go directly over to Hamp's, get a two-
seated sleigh and his best horses, and we will drive over
to T——'s room (for he has some prominent part in their
exercises), pick him up and take him to Newton Inn.
There we will keep him until the night of our banquet,
and he shall respond to a complimentary toast to our
class." Without waiting to hear the deluge of surprised
and chaffing sentences which greeted this, the longest
speech of his life, the man of few words, but much
action, picked up his hat and coat and started rapidly
across the snow-covered campus.

Not more than two good bets had been arranged as to whether it was a bluff, when a "Come on, fellows! Get a hustle!" sounded through the night air.

There was no chance to back out now, even if they had so desired, and within three minutes they were knocking at the door of the luckless Freshman. Being told to come in they did so, and told their victim to prepare for a short drive with them. T—— "tumbled" at once, but, seeing no way of escape, picked up a few necessaries and followed his captors. After a short, but decisive, argument with a few Freshmen who chanced to happen along, and a showing of empty revolvers on both sides, the sleigh was driven rapidly away.

Now a change occurred, and the stranger would no longer have reason to doubt that he was in a college town. From Reed, Thornton, Dartmouth, and all the other dormitories and college rooms, poured a steady stream of excited students, in answer to the alarm of the Freshmen who had seen the kidnapping; and soon there might be seen on every corner knots of excited Freshmen and complacent Sophomores discussing the affair.

The leaders of the Freshman class were not long inactive, and within less than half an hour four sleighs were being driven at top-speed in as many different directions. Long after midnight, however, they returned, unsuccessful, but not entirely discouraged.

The next day passed with the same result. But, meanwhile, the "powers that be" had forbidden the Sophomore class supper, unless the luckless Freshman should be delivered within a few hours, this side up with care.

But no move was made toward returning him, and it began to look like a rebellion on a small scale, as preparations for both suppers were going steadily forward.

How it all ended, and without rebellion, can perhaps best be shown by looking in upon the same trio of Sophomores gathered around the same open fireplace. They were complacently discussing the great success of the scheme of their chum, the man of few words, and wondering if he was enjoying his duty of guarding the Freshman, when suddenly he broke in upon them, his coat torn, his hair dishevelled, and his bleeding face wearing a disgusted look.

To the numerous eager and excited questions hurled at him he would only respond, "Swiped back by six Freshmen." Sitting down at his desk he wrote rapidly for a few minutes, then, tossing the paper to his friends, went out of the room without another word, leaving them to read the following resolution, which was unanimously adopted by the class the next morning:

"Resolved: That a committee of two be appointed to inform the faculty that their demand in regard to Freshman T—— has been complied with, and that he has returned."

N. L FOSTER, '96.

TO A ROBIN.

CHIEF songster in the chorus of the morn,
  Oft hast thou roused me with thy roundelay,
Ere yet a shape of night had slunk away,
Or yet a blush within the east was born;
So eager thou, glad herald of the dawn,
To wake thy feathered minstrels and essay
To trill the rapturous welcome to the day
With bubbling throats, and banish night forlorn.

O, happy bird, I would thy faith were mine,
That in the storm and darkness I could see
A ray of hope, a hint of dawn, and sing.
I would my heart could feel the light as thine,
For every shade is doubly dark to me,
And only in the sun my fears take wing.

                        F. L. PATTEE, '88.

THE TOWER.

WHEN the class of '85 laid the foundation of the Tower, the Old Pine stood as staunch a tree as the proudest elm that now overlooks the campus. Its scores of winters were borne so lightly that none could, in imagination, look but ten years ahead and see a whitened stump marking the spot where, for a century and a quarter, the old woodland king had so well guarded its charge.

It is singularly appropriate that, in the same year when the third stroke of lightning had at last destroyed the Pine, this tower should be capped on almost the same spot where the tree had stood, for the Tower was in no wise planned as a successor.

So familiar had its figure become on this highest point of the college land, that, were it not for the Tower, the hill where the Old Pine laid down its long and honored life, would look bare indeed.

With President Bartlett the idea of its erection originated. '85 laid the foundation, and '95, the last class to enter under Dr. Bartlett's administration, put on the cap. The total height is seventy-one feet, and a climb up the spiral stairway of eighty-six steps, places before one a living map of the college,—the Athletic Oval, the Campus, the Chapel, the Halls,—all Dartmouth living and moving just beneath.

THE TOWER.

But one accident occurred during **the erection.** When the structure **was about** half completed, **the staging** broke, allowing three workmen to **fall upon the rocks** below. **The** men were all badly bruised, **though only** one of them severely hurt.

The material **of** which the **Tower is** built is hornblend-schist, a native **rock** found nearby in great abundance.

Funds were raised by class taxes. '85 laid the foundations. The next **five classes** added eight feet **each.** '91 added six feet, and '92 the **same number.** '93 and '94 combined, and in the spring of '93 added three and four feet respectively. '94 completed the stone-work, and '95 gave the finishing touches by the addition of a cap twelve feet above this. At the left of the main entrance there has been placed a copper plate bearing the following inscription:

· THIS TOWER,

SUGGESTED BY PRESIDENT BARTLETT,

WAS ERECTED

BY SUBSCRIPTIONS FROM THE CLASSES OF

1885 TO 1895

INCLUSIVE.

F. V. BENNIS, '98.

THE TOWER.

TEN years have sped since first they laid thy base,
  Ten classes gone and now thou art complete;
What awe thy noble majesty awakes
In all who, gazing, tarry at thy feet.

O, happy heart, who first conceived the thought
Of lifting thee upon this rocky hill,
Glad thoughts of him shall ever fill the soul
As long as thou and men remain here still.

Thou waitest like some giant priest of old;
Thy plated breast is turned to the west,
Its jewels' numbers plainly cut in gray,
Which speak the voice of those who love thee best.

Through coming years thine eyes will stretch afar
And look upon these pastures sweet in peace;
The waving river 'mid the distant pines
Will flow away ere yet thy watch shall cease.

Thy kindly face will welcome all who come
To this, the home our Alma Mater keeps;
Thou 'lt gaze upon them as they speed away,
While on thy breast the Alma Mater weeps.

WARREN FENNO GREGORY, '88.

When he who views thee now is bent with age,
When storm and wind have beat on thee in vain,
Perhaps, with heavy step and trembling staff
He'll come and look upon thee once again.

F. H. SWIFT, '98.

LOVE'S ROSES.

SIR TRISTRAM'S sword was brave and keen,
  In the sunlight flashing bright,
But oh! so deathly grim, I ween,
  I could not bear the sight.

Sir Tristram's heart was true and leal,
  So manly, high and bold,
But ah! full like his gleaming steel,
  All stern it seemed, and cold.

And so I took the roses fair
  And wreathed the ghastly blade;
All peacefully it nestled there,
  I no more was afraid.

And lo! the knight, by some sweet art,
  Grew warm to me, and kind;
I little knew that 'round his heart
  The flowers of love I twined!

W. F. GREGORY, '88.

A Table

GIVING the date of erection, or purchase, **of all the** regular college buildings **from the beginning**, the purposes for which they **have been used, the dates of their** destruction, etc.

1770. First log hut built. It was about eighteen feet square, and stood at first about ten rods west of the house on Main street now owned by Miss McMurphy. It was soon moved, because of lack of water, to a spot just north of Reed Hall and west of Thornton, and occupied by the family of the president, and, after his house was built, by his servants. Demolished about 1782.

1770. Wheelock's first house built. It was of boards, one story high, with an attic; 40 feet by 32 feet and 10 feet high in the posts. It was originally built near the log hut, and at once moved to a spot on the present common, about two rods south-west of the well. It fronted the south. In 1774, by the help of the citizens, thirty feet, with a belfry, was added at the west end. The eastern third was then used for a commons, and a "lean-to" kitchen added on the north side. The rest was made into a large room, used by the College and citizens for chapel, meeting-house, and public hall. This was the famous "College Hall." Torn down by the students in 1790.

ROBERT HUNTINGTON FLETCHER, '96.

1770. A "school-house" of unknown location and history built.

1770–1771. First College **Hall built.** It was of wood, two stories high, with an attic; 80 feet by 32 feet. It stood in the south-east corner of the present common, facing east. Contained: student's rooms; the preparatory department; until 1774 the commons department; probably a room for the Sabbath services of the church and the public exercises; after awhile the library; perhaps a store until 1773. Taken down in 1791.

1784–1791. Dartmouth **Hall built.** See page 13. Has contained: always — student's and recitation rooms: at times — College library, 1791 (?) –1828 in front middle room, second story, now a part of "Old Chapel," 1828–1840 in whole north end of first floor, unified for that purpose; 1791 (?) –1840 libraries of Social Friends and United Fraternity, in south end, second floor; till 1828, museum in front middle room, third floor, now a part of "Old Chapel"; 1799–1811, Medical department, first in north-east corner, then in whole northern end and south-east corner of present "Old Chapel"; from 1828, "Old Chapel." ?–1836, present North Latin room was divided into "Junior" and "Senior" rooms; in 1836 it was unified for society hall of United Fraternity and Social Friends, and south end of first floor, which they had occupied, divided into two recitation rooms. ?–1868, present South Greek room was divided into "Freshman" and "Sophomore" rooms; in 1868 unified. Numerous other changes in recitation rooms from time to time.

1790. First chapel building **erected.** See page 13. Moved away in 1828.

1791. First academy building for Moor's School erected on present site of "Moor Hall." Was of two stories; rather large, with a porch and belfry (possibly added later). Contained: till 1828, Moor's School, then private schools unconnected with the College; 1794–1801, in second story, printing office. Thoroughly repaired in 1804. Sold and moved away about 1837.

1807. College purchased Col. Kinsman's house. Built near present site of Rollins Chapel in 1791 for Commons hall. Used as such 1791–1793 and 1807–1815. Used also for student's rooms. Apparently destroyed about 1815.

1811. Medical building erected with funds furnished by the State and by private subscription. Has contained students' rooms, lecture rooms, etc. Repaired in 1872–1873. New dissecting room added, 1894.

1828. Wentworth Hall built. Has contained: always, students' rooms; from 1868, North Mathematical room; from 1869, South Mathematical room.

1828. Thornton Hall built. Has contained: always, students' rooms; 1867–1892, in north-east corner, lower floor, rooms of Theological Society and Society of Inquiry, (since 1882, Y. M. C. A.); 1871–1892, on first floor, rooms of Thayer School; from 1893, recitation rooms.

1830 (about). College obtained part ownership of the "College" Church, acquiring right to use galleries and some pews in body. Church built 1796 by private subscription. Had no blinds or arrangements for heating. In 1822, stove introduced; in 1828, radically renovated; from 1867–1869, repaired, carpeted, furnace put in, and entry-ways **on sides added; in 1877, ten feet** added **to rear,** and organ moved **from rear of gallery** to position on **left of** pulpit, college purchased many pews and rearranged position **of** students; **in 1881,** control passed **formally from** pew-owners to Dartmouth Religious **Society;** in 1889, twelve feet added **with means** furnished **mostly by Hon.** Hiram Hitchcock, who gave a new organ.

1833 (about). **College purchased Brown—formerly Rowley—Hall.** Built about **1815 by Mr. Rowley near** present site of Rollins Chapel, **about east of site of** former **commons hall. Contained: stores and students'** rooms; in second **story a hall** used for chapel exercises (and perhaps recitations) by college during quarrel with **"University," afterward for town hall** (approached **by** exterior **stairs),** later **for a** dancing hall. Named **in** honor **of** President Brown. Apparently sold and repurchased **at least once.** Now residence of Professor Emerson, **on North College street.** Sold and moved away, **in** 1843.

1837 (about). Second **academy building for Moor's** School, later, Chandler Building, now Moor Hall, erected. **Had a belfry, which** was removed when Chandler School thoroughly repaired it in **1872. Has** contained: private **schools; a little** later, **Moor's School;** since 1852 **the** Chandler School, now the Scientific department.

1839–1840. Reed Hall built. Named for Mr. William **Reed, of Marblehead, Mass.,** the chief donor. Has contained: **students' rooms, always on third** floor, and, since 1885, on second; library till 1885; mineralogical collection in south-west corner first floor till 1871, when this was transformed into recitation room; picture gallery till 1885; physical laboratories and recitation rooms on about half of first floor till 1885, since then on whole of first floor.

1854. Shattuck Observatory built with funds given by George C. Shattuck, of the Class of 1803.

1866–1867. Bissell Hall, the Gymnasium, built with funds furnished by George H. Bissell, of New York, of the Class of 1845.

1871. Culver Hall built with funds furnished by Hon. David Culver and wife, and the state. Belonged to College and the New Hampshire Agricultural College jointly till 1893, when the College purchased the whole, the amount due to the Agricultural College, through the state ($15,000), having been remitted by vote of the Legislature of 1893.

1884–1885. Rollins Chapel built. The gift of Hon. Edward Ashton Rollins, of Philadelphia, of the class of 1851, in memory of his father, Daniel G. Rollins; his mother, Susan B. Rollins, and his wife, Ellen H. Rollins. Memorial windows of the deceased Presidents of the College have been placed in the chancel and in the transepts.

1884–1885. Wilson Hall built. The gift of Mr. Geo. F. Wilson, of Providence, under the suggestion of his legal adviser, the Hon. Halrey J. Boardman, of the class of 1858. This hall is used for the Library, and also holds the picture gallery until such time as a separate building may be secured.

1885–1895. Tower built, by subscriptions from the College classes. See page 146.

1889–1893. Mary Hitchcock Memorial Hospital built by Hon. Hiram Hitchcock of Hanover.

1890–1892. Y. M. C. A. building erected **with funds raised by** President Bartlett, in honor of whom **it was** named Bartlett Hall in 1893.

1892. College purchased Conant Hall from Agricultural College. **Built in 1873** and named for Hon. **John Conant, of Jaffrey, who** gave most **of** the money for it. **Renamed Hallgarten, in honor** of Julius Hallgarten, **of New York, a benefactor of** the college.

1892. Thayer School purchased **Experiment Station from Agricultural College. Built in 1888 with** funds given by the State.

1894. Professor Sanborn's house entirely remodelled, **transformed** into dormitory, and named Sanborn Hall.

1895. Building of Butterfield **Museum** commenced. A **Museum of** Paleontology and kindred sciences donated by **Dr. Ralph Butterfield, of** Kansas City, occupying the centre of the new quadrangle. See page 132.

R. H. Fletcher, '96.